THE VENGEANCE OF GWA

A Fantasy of Prehistory

I0525716

by

S. FOWLER WRIGHT

WRITING AS "ANTHONY WINGRAVE"

The Borgo Press
An Imprint of Wildside Press LLC

MMVIII

CONTENTS

CHAPTER ONE

BWENE sat in his cave, where none but he would venture to come, unless by invitation from him, even though he should have sat with an open stone, for that was his will, long known and proclaimed aloud in the Cave of Words; and he was King of all the Baradi race, and life and death were the gifts he had power to deal to those who should please or offend his will.

He was King of all the Baradi, the people of the coast flats, who were a numerous folk, dwelling on a narrow stretch of land between the steep cliffs and the sea. They had no footing on the high plain, for it was there that the ape-men dwelt, and would have met them with rending fangs; nor was there much to tempt them to such a strife, for the high plain was barren and dry, and beyond were the frozen hills.

It may be asked why the high plain was not watered from the snow of the frozen hills, but that was simple to see, for at the foot of the mountain range there was a valley, and a chain of lakes, narrow and long, and these were drained by streams that ran seaward through caves that were underground, or emerged into deep canyons that split the plateau in places from east to west.

The plateau was wide enough to have sustained a great people had it been fertile of soil, but it was barren, and, except at one time of year, it had little comfort of rain. The ape-men did not dwell on its surface, but in its higher fissures, into some of which was drained such moisture as the plain would yield. They could not dwell in the valley of narrow lakes, for it was a lava'd land, where nothing grew but a rock plant of a creeping prickly kind, which poisoned a treading foot, so that t would grow purple and swell, and must be cut off with speed if it were not to bring the whole man to the like colour, and bloated death.

Further south, beyond the Baradi land, there was a great river, and on its other bank was forest, rich and fertile and low, into which a blue-black people had come at a former day, and had slain the

5

Baradi who dwelt there at that time, being great of stature and limb. They might have come further, and made an end of a weaker race, but there was little to tempt thereto, they having won the more desirable land. So the King of the Baradi of that day had bought his peace with a tribute of fish, and of skins of seals.

The Ho-Tus (for that was the name which the blue-black people gave to themselves) had gained a land that was fertile and full of game. It had great trees, where men could build high platforms, and roof them with ready boughs, as it had been their habit to do. But that had since changed with the years, as they found themselves to be lords of a land where nothing lived with strength to dispute their power, and they built wooden houses upon the ground....

The King's cave was not fully light, even near its outer end, for the entrance was blocked by a large stone, which was so placed that, when it was closed, it could only be moved from within. There was a space through which light and air came, but it was much too small for a man to squeeze through, even though he were smoothed with fat, so that Bwene could sleep in a better peace than a king should reckon to do.

When he rose with the coming of dawn, as he mostly did, he would pull back the stone, and go forth; but if he willed to think first, he would let it be, and men might say he slept if they would. May not a king sleep when he will?

Now he pondered long in a troubled mind, but his thoughts were not on the Ho-Tus, with whom there was peace so long as the tribute was promptly paid, nor on the ape-men, who had always left the Baradi alone; neither, it may be, being confident of a greater strength, or not having enough desire for a land that was not theirs to try the ordeal of blood.

His thought was on a plague that possessed the land, and on the causes from whence it sprang, whether from the wrath of the gods, or the devices of weaker powers....

It was the law that the King might have but one child, and he a boy. If a girl were first-born, then she must be slain in a public way. If a boy were born, then no other must be allowed to live, unless he should die by some evil chance, when the King might have a new heir, but never two at one time.

It was a very wise and ancient law, for it was told by those of the Sacred Cave that there had once been two brothers who were the sons of a dead king, and who had quarrelled over the rule, and they had promised rewards to men who would take their sides, so that there had been a great folly of strife, and men had died for no gain, till those who remained alive must take the burden of three wives, if not four, that the tribe might be raised anew.

That was not a road to walk twice. And it is easy to see that if there be women left alive of the King's blood, they may think their own sons would be fit to rule, and put evil thoughts in their hearts, from which discords grow. And though the life of a single heir may fail, it is smaller risk, for the land may choose another king to content its will.

Now the King looked back in his mind, and he saw a day when Huni had come to his cave, saying: "The Queen has a female child." And he had answered, as was the law: "Let it be drowned in the sight of all on the third day."

He had not said this with a glad mind, but he had known that, though it might seem to more foolish men that he had an absolute power, yet the ancient customs were far stronger than he.

If he should defy such a law, men would still go their own ways, being moved thereby to resist his will, and he would be a lesser king at the next dawn. But while he followed the ancient laws, as though in a willing way, men did not see the limits that hedged him in.

And so a three-days' child had been drowned on the third day. But that it had been his own—he was not sure. He had had a reason to doubt. And he knew that Bira was not one who would be docile to yield her child, either for an old law or a distant god, if she could contrive in another way.

But the years had passed, and Bira had had no second babe, so that it had seemed that the gods had been stirred to passion, and cursed her womb. And the day had come when he had married a second wife, that there should be an heir for the land when he came to die. She had not been one on whom Bira could look with jealous regard, but a day had come when she had said: "I am with child," and the next week she had gone. None had seen her go, nor had her bones ever been found. She had become no more than an empty place.

The King had looked at Bira in doubt, wondering what she might know, but he had not asked, for, had the girl died by her hands, he would but be met with a bold lie; and had she gone to death by another road, he had had no wish to show that he had such a thought in the dark caves of his mind.

And with the next year he had married another wife. Gwa might lack the bold style of the Queen, but she was a lover of life, and not one who would be expected to disappear in a dumb way. Nor was she one whom those who knew her would soon forget. A time had come when she said: "I have been with child for two months, but have feared to speak. Lord, keep me from the Queen's eyes."

He saw that laughter had left her heart, but though he had questioned long, he could find no substance behind her charge. "That," he had said, "if there be cause, I suppose that I shall be sufficient to do."

And after that Bira had shown the face of a friend to the younger wife, and it may be that her fear had died. But when she had been six months with child, there had come a day when she had been no more than an empty place, and no one had seen her bones.

From that day he had continued a childless king.... And now a fresh plague had fallen upon the land.

CHAPTER TWO

TWO thousand miles from where the Baradi dwelt there was a great city, splendid with opal walls, where a people lived who cared nothing for outer things, or for the savage life which might run over the surface of barbarous lands. They had long conquered all the evils which plague mankind. They had no lack of delectable things.

They had vanquished pain, and made death no more than a pleasant dream, that will come to those who begin to yawn for the night. The beatitudes would have had no meaning for them, who neither quarrelled nor mourned.

Once, in its tenth year, each child was exposed to heat and cold, to hunger and pain, on the outside of the walls, and he would not ask to feel them again, having had enough of the outer things.

The city was very great in itself, but not of such girth as was the sand-blown desert that closed it round, and kept it secure from men of less excellent kinds. Those who ruled in its walls had but one fear (if that could be called by so strong a name which watchful prudence controlled), that love of change, or some folly of discontent, should destroy the heaven-on-earth that their fathers made.

To avert this peril, they ruled all that the young were taught in a most absolute way, choosing only those for full knowledge who could be trusted to use it well.... The Informer made her report on the girls who had come to the end of their nineteenth year.

She said: "Of the fifty girls of the year, there are two who may be placed with those who should be given the fuller course, and one who showed discontent. The others are well content with the pleasures the body gives, and that their desires will be freely fed."

"As to the one who shows discontent," the Controller replied, "she can be spared with a placid will, for there was, as you know, a surplus birth of a year ago, of which adjustment has been delayed, in our over-merciful way, until such a chance as this should arise. You will give her the usual choice."

The Informer returned to the girl, whose name was Raina, and said: "While I was informing you of your last course, it was plain at times that you were less than pleased with the Heaven in which you live."

Raina did not deny that. She said: "I call it fair in a flowerless way, but I suppose that there may be better things which we are likely to miss."

"If you think thus," the Informer replied, "there is one thing that is sure, which is that you are now where you should not be, for we can have no discord to break our peace. But we will deal with you in the merciful way which is provided for such cases as yours.

"We offer you the kindly refuge of death, which, as you know, is open to all as their pleasures tire, and is so contrived that it may be no less than a last ecstasy of delight; or you can be transported, if you prefer, to some distant part of the barbarous earth, where you may learn the meaning of hunger and fear and pain in more detail than you have yet done. And in a year's time, but not less, you may return, if you can, and if you have then come to a better mind.

"You will be sent naked into the world, if you make that choice, leaving even the clothes which now defend you from knowledge either of heat or cold. You can go if you will, but you will be much wiser to die, while you can do it here in a painless way."

Raina said: "Those who live here have the choice of two deaths, either long or slow. But I am choosing to live till the day I die."

CHAPTER THREE

RAINA looked round on a land that was level and bare, and as yellow as a lion's skin. It had a withered stubble, as of a growth that had died, or been grazed away, but it had no suggestion of any resources for clothes, or water, or food. She did not like what she saw. Nor had she comfort in her own state. She felt naked, and, for no more than the second time in her life, she was conscious of cold.

"I suppose," she said, "I might have gone to death by a better way." But her thought changed with the sound of the spoken word, for it roused a small, tawny, fox-like animal almost from beneath her feet. It gave her one startled glance, which showed no surprise, but rather a familiar fear. It fled fast, taking a zigzag course, and was lost to her sight almost at once, on a plain that was coloured so like itself.

She thought: "It has a knowledge of men. Knowledge and fear. There must be those who dwell in these parts, and they have dominion over the beasts, even though they be of the barbarity which the Informer would have me believe. That may be well. But where can I get clothes?"

That was not easy to say, and the question died as it came, for there was a sharp cry of terror from the direction in which the creature had fled. It was zigzagging across her path, unconscious of herself before the impulse of a more certain danger.

Something—was it man or dog?—something larger than itself was in close pursuit—was on it with a final bound, almost before her feet. She saw that the man's jaws—was it baboon or man?—had closed upon the back of the creature's neck. There was a moment's scuffle, and it was being shaken violently from side to side, as a dog shakes a rat (though the disparity of size was much less) till it hung limply from the lifted mouth.

The mouth of what? Was it man or baboon or dog? It was hard to say. But no—not dog. The idea had come with the dog-like pursuit of a flying prey, but it was a resemblance that lessened with a closer view. The face was more human than that of a dog; more human than that of a baboon, though the line of nose and forehead were one. That was the difference that divided it from the human kind—the forehead receded backward following the line of the nose. The body was dark brown, but hairless. More human than baboon in that also. He stood on all fours, on straight arms, and on legs that bent outwards in a curious way, adjusting their difference of length, but a moment later he rose erect without difficulty, though his knees bent outward. That was when he first saw she was there. Before that he had torn the body with strong teeth, and drained its blood with a sucking sound, not pleasant to hear. Most unpleasant for one who might be the next object of that swift pursuit.

The ape was looking her way…looking with black-red, fiercely-intelligent eyes. Now that it had risen erect, it was of something more than her own height, in spite of the outward-bending knees…. Its gaze did not seem to be of an active threat, though it was not friendly at all. It was puzzling, unexpected, in a way that she could not define.

She stood quietly still, not attempting the folly of useless flight.

Yet when it advanced upon her, step by step, still remaining erect, she withdrew at a similar pace. She was careful not to show haste or fear, but she could not easily endure that this creature should touch her flesh, perhaps paw her over, perhaps feel her with a smelling muzzle, perhaps tear her with sudden jaws, perhaps…. No, she could not avoid the implications of those retreating steps.

But, seeing her so withdraw, he did not attempt to come close, as he might have done. Rather he moved aslant till he was nearly at her other side. Then he advanced again. Soon she perceived what it meant. He did not wish to close in upon her. He did not wish to frighten her into a run. She was being driven—gently driven, as one might shepherd a timid hen…. Driven where, and for what?

They went on thus for half a mile, or it might be more. The drained, flaccid body of the dead creature had been left on the ground. Evidently it was the blood, not the flesh, which the ape (for so she had named him now) had desired. She was easy to drive. There was no sense in dodging to left or right. It would be the same at last, and she would have tired herself to no useful end. She had more sense than a fowl. Perhaps it might be well that the ape should perceive that. Learning the way it would have her go, she went as straight as she could, and was turned with ease. So they came to a new sight.

They came to a sudden gap in the plain. It did not end there. They looked across, and it was the same as before. They looked down, and there was a canyon beneath their feet, a canyon more deep than wide, though it was of some width. Beyond that, it seemed that the plain went on to the sky's fall, though it might be with other cracks such as that into which she gazed. What was she to do now?

It seemed that she was to descend, which was not easy to think. The side of the canyon was steep. There was no path. There was no growth to which weight could hang. She could not climb like an ape. Yet she did what she must, as we mostly do.... Once she scratched her leg on a stone. A long scratch on the outer side of the left calf. A mere breaking of skin. But it bled. She had a panic thought that her captor might be roused by the sight of blood to a new thirst. She went the faster for that. She tried to move so that it should not be seen.... She tried to wipe the blood off with a furtive hand.... Then they came to a gentler slope, and to a place of trees that rose from a sandy soil.

Here her captor stopped, with a barking cry, which was yet rather a voice than a bark. It was answered by varied sounds of the same kind. That it was language was easy to perceive, though it might be of a poor sort.... Now she was surrounded by apes in the gathering dusk.... It was almost dark under the trees, though they were not of a dense shade, being of lank growth and a somewhat feathery top. They might have been hybrids of the Australian gum and a desert palm. They were unlike either of these, yet the two may give an impression of what they were. But that is how that would look on the next day. She had more urgent thoughts at this time than the observation of trees that it was too dark to see well.

She was being driven into a low tunnel of living boughs, or so she thought, making a good guess in the dusk. They were boughs that met overhead, so that she must stoop a little, lest she be caught by the hair. She went but three or four yards by this way, and came into a walled and covered place. She heard behind her a rustling of thorns, and the passage darkened as it was closed.

She stood still, seeing nothing at first. Then she thought that there were those, either beasts or men, who crouched under the further wall. Well, she would stay where she was, till the light came. So far, she was unharmed. That might be because she had had the wisdom not to resist.

She would lie on the floor and rest. She would have found covering if she might, but how was that to be done? She stepped on something that was small and soft, and that gave way under her foot.

She drew it back in a sudden doubt, and was on others of the same kind. But they did not squirm or withdraw. Probably they were harmless, and not alive.... In the end, she found a clear place, and lay down. She did not wake till the dawn came.

CHAPTER FOUR

SHE opened bewildered eyes to the dimness of a place that was not windowed at all, but that was walled and roofed with twisted bundles of thorn through which some light came. There were five other creatures of about her own size caught in the same cage (if cage it were), and as the light strengthened they began to move about, and to pick up from the floor.

Now she saw that they were of the ape-kind, alike to those that had driven her here. Was she in the public jail? Or might it be that she was not jailed at all, but in a kindly hospitality? It was hard to tell.

But she was hungry, and her thirst was great. What did they pick and eat from the floor? She perceived that it was a small oblong fruit, date-like in shape, but having a blue-black skin, which was scattered freely about. Doubtless it was some of these on which she had trodden last night. How different things look in the day!

She did not like to take a meal from the floor. But she liked to starve even less than that. That which was good for these other creatures should sustain her own life. She found it to be a fruit which would peel. It had a good taste. She ate, and had a worse thirst than before. But she could see nothing to drink.

The other creatures were round her now, having finished their own feeding, and having perceived her to be different from themselves. They surrounded her in a half circle, as she sat with her back to (but not touching) the thorny wall. They seemed curious rather than hostile, discussing her in their own tongue. They were particularly curious to see behind her shoulders, peering from either side between her back and the thorny wall. She was puzzled by this till she noticed that each of them had a yellow oval mark below the back of its neck, and perceived that they looked to see if she were branded in the same way, and were surprised that she was not.

After a time, they lost interest in her, sitting about the floor in a listless way.

She considered them in the growing light, and thought that they were a poor lot. There was one male, old and with a scarred and lustreless skin. He had lost an ear. There were four females, of which two also were old, though they looked vigorous enough in a dried-up way. One of the others had a face that was deformed, or had been distorted by accident or disease, very evil to see. The last was well-formed and young, out of a savage aspect—the only one (she thought) to be feared. What could it all mean? As to that, she was getting too thirsty to care. Let them give her water, and they could do what else to her they would. Did they never drink?

She wondered, were they of the nature of men? If she could communicate her need to their minds, would it rouse them to sympathy, or a possible help? She tried this, pointing to her mouth, and making signs as of one who drinks. She raised cupped hands. She made a sucking sound. She tried other symbols. She thought that she was understood, but their reaction was strange and hostile. It was as though the suggestion of water were an indecent or repulsive thing. They drew back, chattering. The young female that she was disposed to fear snarled. She felt that if she did not desist, there might be teeth at her throat. At the thought, her own jaw tightened in a way which was new and strange, but it was a strife that she did not seek. She sat still.... Perhaps she had been wrong to think of them as a kind of man. Most of the earth's mammals are content to control themselves to circumstance, but men seek to control circumstance to themselves. By this reckoning she might call them men of a kind, but the distinction is not absolute. There have been other creatures, among insects if not mammals, in every age, who have made their own world. There are mammals and birds that have their individuality, their adaptability, though limited by the greater isolation of their lives, they not having learned to record their thoughts to communicate them from generation to generation. Broadly, the distinction is of degree, not of kind.... But there are very few creatures that do not drink!

Now there were noise and movement outside, and the barrier of the entrance was pulled away. Three of her captors came in, entering on all fours. They sat round her, talking. Their speech seemed to be of vowel sounds, running up and down a musical scale in a barking way, very strange to hear. She doubted that she would ever learn to understand such a tongue, and to speak it would be harder still.

The one that had caught her sat in the midst. He seemed to her in control, though the other two were males as finely formed as him-

16

self. The other captives, withdrawn to the further wall, looked to be of a very meagre aspect in this comparison.

Well, if she could not understand their speech, she must try that they should understand hers. She made the same signs of thirst as before. She looked in fear of a similar hostile reaction, but it did not come. They watched, but she could tell nothing of their thoughts.

And then—too suddenly to resist—the apes that were on either side reached forward and seized her arms. They drew her on to her face before the one who sat in the midst. She struggled for freedom, and it was all so instant that it seemed that she had come clear at the first pull. She sat up, and they were all as they were. But between her shoulder blades there was a sharp pain. That she had been branded, as were the others, was a thing easy to guess, though she could not tell what it might mean.

Her thoughts returned to the thirst which was even more; insistent than the pain that her shoulders felt. If she could have made them understand that! But they were already gone, and the entrance was being closed.

She felt desperate then. She considered the thorny walls. She saw that they were not formed of separate boughs, but of whole bushes of thorn which had been closely pressed. It was a forbidding wall. Yet freedom is worth a price. It is worth much to one who thirsts, as she did. Would the others interfere? She must try the event. She would have waited till night, but she was sure that she could not break through that barrier in the dark.

Handling the thorns with care, she broke off one or two fragments. These were absurdly small, but the thorns were large and closely set, having a broad base, like those of a briar, but of a worse kind. Then she scratched her wrist. It was a tiny scratch, of which she took no heed. Trying to pull away a length of thorn, it rebounded against her arm. It left several punctured wounds on the upper arm of which she would have taken less heed had not her wrist throbbed. It was hot to touch. She saw that they were poisonous thorns. Poisonous to her, if not to her companions. How much so she would soon know. She stopped work, watching her wrist. The others took no notice at all. They may have known that what she did was a futile thing.

As she sat thus, her wrist and arm becoming hotter, and somewhat swollen, though not as much as she had feared at first, the entrance was opened again. None came in, but there was a cry without which the others clearly understood. They rose, with an aspect of sullen reluctance, but without hesitation. They went out, and she followed. There was more hope in any change than in sitting there.

Outside she came to a stronger light. It was nearing noon. There was a clear space between the trees and the thorn-hut which she had left. She saw a number of male apes that stood round, erect on their hind legs. They might be spectators or guards. There were six wicker baskets on the ground. They were shaped to fit the back, somewhat like a fisherman's creel, being curved on the inner and more on the outer side. There were shoulder straps and a lower one for the waist. They had a watertight lining of some thin light metal inside, and an inner lid of the same. She saw that these apes must be creatures who could plan and work. Seeing that the others were putting on the baskets, though in a sullen way, she did the same. The significance of the number was easy to read. She had no will to make trouble by disobedience, at least till she could better tell what it all meant. Perhaps these were no other than slaves, or criminals condemned to some distasteful work. It was beyond possibility to guess what it might be, but any change gave hope. There might be water where she would go.

Then, with the suddenness of a cat, the young female sprang—she of the savage eyes. She sprang at a male ape who stood watching her, somewhat behind the rest. It was so sudden that none could interpose. He had no time even for the instinctive lifting of hands that would be a guard to his own throat. They rose swiftly indeed, but it was to tear at teeth that already met. He went down from the impact of the spring, and as he did so she drew back. She rose up, well content, from a dying thing.

There was outcry to left and right. The young female made no motion either to fight or fly. One who had stood at the side of the dying ape lifted a wooden spear. In another moment, it would have revenged the deed, but, on an impulse strange to herself, Raina struck it aside with the basket which she was lifting to adjust to her own back.

She was puzzled afterwards as to why she had done this. She had no cause to take the part of a murderess who was not of her kind, and who had shown no kindness to her. It would have shown a depth of folly to engage in aggressive action in such a cause. But she had not done that. Indeed, though of a restless curiosity which had brought her there, she was not of aggressive character. She had only intervened to save life from a sudden thrust. Perhaps there was some faint obscure impulse springing from the fact that they appeared to be in a common slavery, bearing a common brand. Perhaps it was a memory of the look of satisfied and derisive hate which she had seen in the dead ape's eyes, and which had met that swift and deadly reply. Anyway, so it was.

And, as is often the issue of that from which prudence turns, but which courage does, for herself it seemed to have no consequences. That it saved the life of the female ape for that time was a certain thing. For there was no second blow. There was swift clamour of sounds. There was order made. It seemed that they were to adjust their baskets and to go on, and the murderess also, as though she had done nothing at all. Raina saw that he who struck would have been very willing to strike again, but he was overruled by reason, or by those with more power than himself. Was it that the fate to which they six were doomed was so dreadful that no punishment could be worse?

They went on under the trees which she now saw clearly for the first time. They went down the course of the canyon, following a single path, one after one. There was none to guide, the old scarred male going first, though there were those who followed behind. Raina saw from this that they must walk in a known way, and with some measure of their own consent. Anyway, she was last of the six. To one who walked on so blind a path there was some comfort in that.

The path descended in a very gradual way. Always aware of the thirst that ached in her throat, she looked ever for pool or stream, but she saw none.

When they had gone for about two miles, there was a patter of rain among the leaves. Those who were ahead halted at that, as though being unwilling to go on. But those who walked in the rear cried to them in an angry way. The patter ceased. They went on as before.

Then there was heavier rain, which was not quick to stop. Those in front halted again. There was hesitation now among those who drove them from the rear. They would not let the line turn back, but they did not urge it ahead. So it stood, and was drenched.

As for Raina, she had thought but for one thing. She caught rain in her joined hands. She licked rain from bare arms. She sucked rain from around her lips with a stretched tongue. When they were allowed to turn after a time, she scarcely knew what she did, being in such bliss from that storm. The rain streamed over her naked body from head to foot. She felt she was breathing rain.

As they laid down the baskets in the place where they had taken them up, the one whose life she had saved from a spear's point was

19

at her side. She saw her look at a place where a dying body had kicked but two hours ago. It was gone now, but there was a wide space of blood on which the rain beat. The young ape looked at this with a snarling lip, making a face which was not pleasant to see, but Raina was content enough. She felt it to be the face of a friend, and of a fellow slave with a branded back. But what, she asked again, did it all mean? For what purpose had they set forth, which was so clearly dreaded, and which yet could be turned back by a shower?

Being shut up as before, her companions began to search the ground for such fruit as was left, which was not much. Raina's thirst being stayed, she found that she had hunger enough, but she would not scramble for that which (she thought) had lain on the ground too long. She was rewarded for that reluctance when one came and brought a fresh supply of the fruit, which he bore in a fibre bag. The bag was not new, and it burst as he would have scattered its contents on the ground. Seeing that, he cast it down, as a thing used.

Having eaten her need, she looked at the bag, and had a thought. She enlarged the hole which had burst in the bottom till her head would go through, though her shoulders would not pass it with ease. She did not want it too large. In the end, she had a skirt, at which she was better pleased than at the best dress she had ever bought. It had come to her by a strange unlikely chance, but with so much ill fortune being hers, was it not fair that there should be some small thing in the other scale? There was no lifting in the cloud of her greater need. She listened in the night for the sound of a rain which did not come.

Still, there must be fresh water somewhere. She had felt rain.

When would they let her loose? She had no words, and they would not understand signs.

She considered the one whose life she had saved, and of whom she now thought as a friend. She was sitting by herself now. She had a savage jaw, but her expression was more content than before, as of one who had done that which she would. If she could make her understand, she might tell them. They couldn't *want* her to die of thirst. But it was not easy to see how she could explain it by signs, and she remembered how strangely, in what a hostile way, her previous pantomime had been received. She did not wish to convert a friend to a new enmity.

While she hesitated, the entrance was opened again. Once more they were released that they might take up the burdens of the baskets, and the procession of yesterday was repeated. Raina looked up to a sky which was hot and blue. It was near to noon, and the sun shone down into the gorge. She could see no hope of rain. She thought that her companions looked upward with a like hope and were as disappointed as she, and from the same cause.

There was one other incident of a disconcerting kind as they started out, which she endured with a wise passivity. When she had been inspected before by the ape population (which was not more than three score in all, in this place, as far as she could observe) they had shown some curiosity, though perhaps less than there might have been. Now that she walked out in the greater assurance of the acquired skirt, she had a different experience. They crowded close to look. They pulled it up to observe what it might mean or hide. In the end they decided that there was nothing there. So she was allowed to go on.

CHAPTER FIVE

THE gorge widened somewhat, and bent sharply to the left. As it bent, the scene changed. The trees, which had gradually become smaller and more scattered, ceased, and there was a bare rocky slope. On the left, another gorge joined that by which they had come, the two uniting in this bare descent, which ended abruptly at the side of a wider and far deeper canyon which crossed their front.

On the edge they must halt. Behind them were the two converging gorges: on either hand were sheer walls of rock: before them was sheer descent: opposite was the further wall of the great canyon into which they looked.

Looking over the edge of that sheer descent, Raina saw the floor of the canyon. It was edged by a growth of trees that looked like bushes, being so far down, and there was a river, running fast, that shone in the midday sun.

Here was water enough for a nation's thirst, had it been possible to descend that wall—which was a vain thing to dream. Why had they come?

Raina looked to the opposite wall of rock which rose to a like height to those which were on either hand, and she saw that the level which she had first known must be a great tableland of the earth, flat and barren and very high, which these fissures rent; only, the two gorges which were behind her were of a less depth, while this into which they led went down to the very bottom of a lower land.

They were moving now to the left hand, the old male going first, as he had from the start, but she could not guess what they would do, for it was but a space of ten yards along the land's edge, and then they came to the wall of rock which they could not climb. Could they go out on the cliff's face? It was wild to dream, it being almost sheer and at so dizzy a height, though it was what she would have had a will to do, had it been more gentle of slope, for there was a stream of water that broke out from its side, it might be forty yards away, or a little more, somewhat higher than where they stood, and

22

fell in a cascade down the precipitous side, so that it seemed to her sight that it ended as a mere mist in the air before it reached the depth to which it was ever flung.

The side of the cliff was not smooth, though it fell so sheer, but was of a rocky surface, rough and broken and hard, and covered in places by a small mossy falling plant of a blackish-green colour, having blue flowers, bright but very small. As she looked more closely she saw, not a path—for how could it be called that where there was no level on which the feet might tread?—but the faint marks of a traversed way. It was no more than a blurring of the mossy growth, an accenting of places where foot must have followed foot, or where the hollow above a rocky knob had been deepened by the holding of many hands, and as she saw this, she saw too that it was the way that they were meant to take, for the old male had stepped out and was clinging with hands and feet to the cliff's face, while her remaining companions sat down along the edge, waiting their turn, for it was clear that it was not such a path as two could take at one time, which would have meant that they must cross as the first returned.

So she sat and watched, thinking of what it must mean, and of what she would do when her turn came.

As to what it might mean, that was becoming easy to see. If there were no water in these high gorges, or on the tableland overhead, and it must be fetched at this peril of life at times of a long drought, then it might be a natural thing that they should condemn the old to this risk, for they were no loss when they fell, and it might well be that they would add to these such as were of an ill temper or an ill build, which they could lightly spare, and that one captured from they knew not where (meaning herself) might be put to the same use. But what she should do was a harder thing to resolve.

She was not one who was overmuch feared of a great height, as many are, but her limbs were not trained to hold to a cliff side as a fly walks. Besides, she saw that what she did once, she might be expected to do again and again. And the end of that would be a most certain thing.

If she should refuse the attempt at first, it was a thing which they could not force her to do. That was clear. But how they would act then was a greater doubt. They might throw her over the edge. They might let her go. She might have tried that chance but for the thirst which was in her throat, and that the water was a lure from which it was not easy to turn.

Of course, they might let her drink from that which the others brought, but it was less than a sanguine hope.... In the end, and it was sooner to think than to write, she resolved that she would make the attempt, if the others should come safely back. She would get her drink, and after that she must; escape as she best could. So she watched the one who had gone first, that she might learn what she could.

She saw that he went on safely, moving slowly and with care, even at times with more caution than she would have thought needful, though ever as one without fear, being in control of himself and of that which he did, and so he came to the place where the water fell, and filled that which he bore, and was most of the way back, when there was a warning cry from some of those who watched, at which he stopped, flattening himself against the face of the rock, and clutching hard on such hold as he could gain at that place.

And in the next minute she saw what his fear was, for a huge bird flew toward them up the great gorge, having a spread of wings which there would be no eagles to match. She saw that it was of a glossy black colour, but with a speckled breast, and having a great beak, yellow and hooked. It flew past the clinging man, and struck him with a buffeting wing, turning almost in the act that it might strike him again from the other side. It did not strike with talons or beak, and it was easy to see that its object was to beat him off the place to which he clung, that he might fall to his death, and be meat in the gorge below.

It must have done this in the end, had not those who saw picked up the lumps of rock that were round their feet, and thrown at it, for which the distance was not too great. They threw hard and straight, and in a short time the great bird had had more than enough, and soared higher, to be free of that shower, and then screamed in an angry way, and made off with a flight that was easy and slow.

After that he who had been in such risk made his way back, and the others were not anxious to take their turns. Their protests were plain enough, even to one who could not speak in their tongue, but they gained nothing thereby. The bird was gone, and it seemed that they must do that for which they came, be they willing or loath. And so, one by one, they did, and Raina watched that they came back alive, and thought she might do the same with a like care, and the water was a strong call (for they had pushed her back with rough hands, and with angry cries, when she would have drunk from that which the others brought), and she saw that when she got to it she could both fill her creel, and drink all that she would.

At this time there had been arrival of another troop of apes from the other gorge, which joined the one by which she had come, where the bend was, and they also brought some who were old or of little count, that they might serve the tribe in the same way.

Seeing these others to wait their turn, and not being one to provoke her captors to no good end, Raina lost no time, but rose to set out, as the last of her companions stepped back to the level ground.

She would not look down, but turned somewhat to the cliff's face, seeking for foothold with steady eyes, and making sure of her grip, by which means she did well enough for the first few yards, and then found she had something to learn which might have cost her life, and which it is likely that she would have been told had she known the apes' speech, or they hers. For she put foot on the mossy trailing growth which hung from the cliff's face, at a spot where it was flat, and had the look of a safe rest, but this moss was of so soft and slippery a kind that her foot shot out to the air, and had she not had a good grasp at that moment she had been but a dead thing. As it was, she shook for a time with a fear which she could not rule, and could do nought but cling to the rock's face, making no effort to move. At that time she had no thought but to go back, be the penalty what it might, but as her heart slackened at last, and her breath took its own speed, she thought again of the thirst which would still be hers, even though they should let her live, if she went back with an empty creel. So at that she went on, though with a greater heed than before, knowing now why it had seemed to her that the others had moved with an even greater caution that she had thought it needful to do.

Moving thus, she came to the place where the water fell, and here she drank long, swallowing all that she might, for she did not know when the next chance would be, except she came here again, and then, having done, she filled her creel, and turned to retrace her way. She had gone but a few steps when she heard a warning cry, such as had been given when the great bird came before, and at that she looked, and had a very terrible fear, for wings came from the higher sky, and those not of one bird, but of two.

There was barking and throwing of many stones, as there had been before, but now they were little more than a vain threat, for the distance was too great, they who threw having to lean out too far for a forceful throw or a good aim, and it was easy to see that there could be but one end.

A great wing struck her arm with a bruising blow, and; before she could regain balance there was another against her side. She was somewhat turned at that, and must look down as she moved to strengthen her grip. She saw a tree that stuck out from the cliff's face. It was far below, but it was further from the ground than from her. It was a meagre tree, of few leaves, but it showed the whiteness of an ape's bones, which were still as he had hung in the tree when he fell. There was no comfort in that.

"But that," she thought, "or the ground below, is where I shall soon be, and I must get there as best I can, for there is no other end." And at that she found that her mind was clear and calm. Her thoughts were rapid, but very cool. It was a wild idea, but a chance. All this was in the space that the birds took to turn. Then they buffeted her again, and she held on with a desperation of bleeding hands.

Before they reached her for a third time, she had loosed the creel from her back, so that, when they smote, it fell clear, and she was the better by the loss of the weight. They wheeled, screaming, at that fall, and then they shot down, faster than the creel fell, to see what it was, and soared upward again with baffled discordant cries.

She used those seconds to move a few feet, gaining a firmer hold, and then she set herself to endure till the time should come which would be her chance.

She was buffeted from left and right till she felt that she was all one bruise, and as they passed they came closer and closer still, till the beak of one grazed her shoulder, so that she could not forbear to loose one hand to beat it away. She saw the great yellow beak and the fierce tawny eyes, exultant with the greed of a prey that was nearly won, and she thought: "It is that one it shall be. But I have missed a chance. I was a coward that time. It shall not be so again." For her thought was that the next time it came so close she would seize it in her arms, and there should be two or none that would fall to the depth below.

So at that she loosened her hold, and turned as far as she might to face the abyss below, but her eyes were not on that depth, but on the wide spread of the wings that were but a few yards away in the level air.

The bird may have thought that she was about to slip, and that he would make an end, for he dashed upon her with a great force, and as he did this she leapt upon him, seeking that her arms should be round his neck.

There was a second when she thought that she was lost indeed, for the great bird swerved with an instant speed, and it was only with one hand that her grasp took. Yet it held till the other arm made

26

a better grip. And then she had a quick joy in the thought that it would be two or none, though she could not tell which it would be.

For they went down fast at the first, or, as it seemed to her eyes, looking over the shoulder of the falling bird, the cliff rose past her at a great rate, but it was a speed that slackened as the great wings beat with a frightened strength, and there was a moment when she must doubt whether it might not even avail to bear her away, but her weight was too great for that.

Down they went, though at a slow speed, and with a new peril for her. For now the bird, having steadied its flight, and understanding better the trouble that pulled it down, became active to cast her off, either by beak or claws. She was bold to loose with one hand, that she might hold its head off with a grasp of the feathered throat, but the claws were a different thing, and twist and kick as she might she was saved at one time only by the rough thickness of the skirt she wore from being torn in the lower parts, in a way that would not have been easy to heal. As it was, there was blood that ran to her foot, though she took no heed of that, having more urgent matters of which to think.

Had that struggle been on the ground, there is little doubt but her death would have been its end, but, as it was, she looked down, and trees and river rose to meet her, being now large and near, and then they struck with a great splash, and when she knew she was safe she loosed her hold, and dived and swam for a reeded bank.

The bird flapped its way to the river shore, with a turmoil of scattered spray, and made off with a cowed flight, low over the trees. The other bird, which had circled down at their own pace, but without taking part in a struggle which it may not rightly have understood, made a swoop at the head which rose as she swam for the reeds, so that she had a doubt whether the peril were yet past, but when it saw that its mate was in retreat, it made off by the same way, and so Raina lay on the river bank, and could get her breath once again, and think of the escape she had had, both from the peril of death, and from the apes that had made her a slave. But there was one ape of which she thought most, a young female with a savage jaw, for as she turned to leap for the bird's neck she had had an instant of sight of one who started to come to her aid at that need, with a wooden spear in her hand.

CHAPTER SIX

OUR present want is ever the greatest, be it whatever it may. An hour before, Raina would have said that water is man's first need, and, if he have that, he cannot be in so evil a case that he should complain overmuch.

Now she lay on a river's bank, and there was more water flowing before her face than she could have drunk in a hundred years, and did she thank Heaven for that? Not at all. Her mind was on other things. She had a wound which would make it a trouble to walk, though she saw that it might have been worse: her single garment was a torn rag, at which she had the less reason to grieve as it had cost her nought: more important, she felt the need of a meal which she did not know how to get. Did she want to go back to the apes? Hardly that. Yet she gave it enough thought to observe that, had she so wished, it might not have been easy to do. She looked round for those tough-boughed trees with which she had become familiar in the upper gorge. She knew that with their fruit, if she could find it, she would do well enough. But that was what she could not do. They grew in a cooler place. On this level to which she had come, there was a heavy warmth in the windless air of the deep gorge, and though there was little growth from a rocky soil, except somewhat at the river's edge, what there was, was of ranker, fleshier sort than had been the trees of the higher cleft.

She looked down the river's way, thinking that if she went by that path she should come to an open land at the last, which might be fertile of fruits where the winds blew at their own will, and the sun had his way with the earth from the dawn to the natural dusk, and it came to her mind to wonder that those apes should dwell in a high place where no water was. Why did they not come down here? It seemed that it must mean that there was no way from the high level of the upper plain to that to which she had come by so strange a fall. That might mean that she must go far between walls that were narrow and high. Still, it had to be proved. It was no use to stay here. It seemed the fainter hope to go up the stream by a narrowing cleft. She must do what she could while the strength was hers, and the light held. So she went down the gorge.

She did not go fast, for one who treads among rocks does not move as though on a level road, and those whose feet are bare will soon learn to look first before the step fall, and she may not have gone as far as she would have guessed, when she came to a place on her left hand, where the fall of the cliff was less sheer, and looking up she was the more amazed that the apes did not come to the water by that way, for the slope lessened even more as it rose, being covered with a dense growth of thorns, such as had been cut to make the walls of the prison in which she had been held for the last two nights. And then she remembered how poisonous were the pricks they gave, and was somewhat less sure.

But she made a better pace in the next hour, it seeming at times that she had the help of a trodden way, and this the more as she went on, so that she grew afraid of what it might mean, saying to herself: "There are those, either beasts or men, who come up the side of this stream. They come upward from below, and the higher it was, the fewer there were who would come that far. What do I go to meet at such haste?" She was afraid, yet she must go on, for there were no means of life where she now was. Only water to drink.

Then she came to one of the palm-fruit trees, which grew from a cleft in the rocky wall, somewhat over her head, and small, as being out of its natural place, but it had dropped some fruit, and she threw rocks, winning more.

She ate what she could, and made shift to carry some, folding the side of her torn skirt, so that they could be held as she walked. She felt better for that meal, and the hope it gave.

Then she went on anew, and came to a place where the walls of the gorge narrowed again, and the stream, which was no wider than it had been at first, or not much, had no more than room to pass with the help of a deeper bed, and a stirred speed. There was little space for her if she would walk dry, and it was here that her mind cast its last doubt—there was a path, trodden and clear, between the stream and the cliff wall.

Now a path may be trodden by many creatures that are not men, and that may be better or worse than they, and she was not one who was used to call a guess by a worse name. Also, unless she would that she should come to a place that was empty of all her kind, a sign of the nearness of men should be that which she should be most glad to meet. Yet this was no less true, that she thought that path to be such a sign, and that she saw it with a heartbeat of dread.

On the first point, she was right in fact, whether by premonition or chance, and as to having reason to fear, well, it is a thing to be judged as the tale moved to its end.

Anyway, so it was. It may have been from the contact she had already had with the apes, which were so near to men, and were yet not (to her) of a pleasant kind, but she looked on the hardness of that narrow path as Crusoe would look on a later day at the print of a man's foot on the sand. She had to call all her courage that she should go ahead by that way, which she did at a slow pace, looking ever to right and left, and starting once when a bird flew.

And so she came to the cave.

They did not see her at first, being too intent on that which they watched in their midst, and she might have passed unseen in a quiet way, but for the steps that were cut down to the stream, which would have been hard to cross except she should push aside him who sat with his back to the topmost edge. But she did not think to do that. She just stood and watched, for it was a strange thing that she saw.

There was a gourd of blood in the midst, and there was a heap of dead birds cast aside, of the size of crows, and as black as they, out of which it was easy to guess that the blood had come; and there were four who bent over the bowl.

The one who sat facing the light at the entrance of the cave, and who might have seen that there was one who watched had she lifted her eyes, was a woman, such as the world (holding many types) might have held in a later day. She was brown and slender and young. Her head was small, even for her size, it being covered with hair that rippled rather than curled and that was of a glossy black at the front and top, but of a more bronze colour at the back and sides. This was a new thing, that the hair on a woman's head should be of two colours (not being dyed, as she did not think it to be), though she saw that it was nothing strange in itself. The eyes of the woman (who was no more than a girl, and may not have come to her full growth) were large, and of a very dark blue, but they were less easy to see, being cast down on the bowl. She was clothed in a close-fitting garment, brightly red, that might be of smooth cloth or a polished skin, out of which her neck rose, and she had a necklet of shining stones.

The three who sat round her were men, darker brown than she, old by the whiteness of their short hair, and by the wrinkles in faces from which no beards grew. Each was clothed alike in a garment of

30

white cloth, broidered with red, and having a red stone at the throat, and a flint-headed club lay near to the hand of each.

There was a heap of wood ash on their side of the bowl. The girl tipped the bowl from side to side in a spinning way, and as she did this each of the men in turn cast a pinch of ash on to the surface of the curdling blood. Each of them did this four times, and then a cloth was cast over the blood, and each shook it in turn. Then the girl lifted the cloth from the bowl, and they bent forward to see the figure which the ashes had made.

Raina could not see this, nor could she interpret their words, or she might have understood that which followed more quickly than she was able to do.

The man who sat in the midst said: "It is a woman's form, and by the line of her breast she is still barren and young. Priestess, it is yourself who must lift this cloud from our tribe."

But the girl said: "You are wrong. She is much taller than I." She seemed to draw back, as one called to a work that she would not be eager to do.

The man said: "It is the Queen?"

She denied this also: "No, it is not she.… It…it is one whom the gods will send in their own time."

The man who sat on the girl's left hand said: "She has her face to the west. She must come down the gorge from the canyon that is empty of men."

As he said this, he looked the way that his thought went, and Raina fronted his gaze. He cried out in a sudden fear, and they all looked, and wonder was in their eyes.

They saw a woman, taller and whiter than they, and with a crown of shortened chestnut hair, such as they had not known, and yet being kin to them, as they to her, in a way in which the ape-men could never be. She wore nothing but a skirt of coarse grey fibre cloth, which in itself was of a god like mode, for their own bodies were fully covered; but what they noticed most was the gathered fruit which she held at her side, in a fold of the lifted skirt, for they knew that it was such fruit as grew in the upper gorges, where the ape-men were, though they knew that there was no path by which they could be reached from that canyon, from end to end, even to where the stream first came from the depths of the rock, issuing from a dark cave, and between walls that were narrow and high.

The girl said: "She has come from the hollow depths, as the stream comes, for there is none like her in all the earth, and there is no other way. She brings the fruit to show us that by which those who are left may live."

The man on her right said: "It may be as you say, for you are nearer the gods than we; but it will avail us nothing at all, the fruit being beyond our reach."

The girl answered to that: "The shore cliffs could be climbed."

The man said: "I did not mean that. Will the apes sit still? Will they come to us to be slain that we may pile them in one heap? Shall we eat that by which they live, and they do nothing at all?"

But the other men cried out: "She will show us how this thing may be done. It is for that she is come. If you speak thus, she may leave us in a great wrath. Have you no child that can die?"

The man shook with fear at that. He answered quickly, as one who would be first in his words: "She will not be wroth, knowing that I meant nothing at all…. Goddess"—he turned to Raina, rising as he did this, so that he might bend his knees in an outward way, doing her all the homage he might—"Goddess, I am a very foolish man."

She made some answer to that, being so directly addressed. It matters nothing what she said, for they could not understand her any more than she them, but at the sound of the strange tongue the girl who was priestess rose. She said to the men: "You can go now. Come tomorrow at the noon hour, and I shall have learned what the gods will us to do."

They went at that without pause, while she came over to Raina, not showing the fear she felt, for a priestess must not show fear before those whom she should rule, and took her hand, saying: "Come with me. There is one within who is wiser than I."

Raina understood the gesture, though not the words, and she was of a mind to understand more. She followed into the cave.

CHAPTER SEVEN

BWENE sat in the shadow at the back of his own cave, for it was there that he had found that he could think best, and he had much matter for thought, in a mind that was aware of its own ignorance (in which he was as ourselves), and which was impeded by the things which he thought he knew (as men will be to the end). He did not know all that we do today, but he knew that the divinations of those who dwelt in the Cave of Ghosts (which was an old name by which the Sacred Cave was once known) were not to be lightly weighed.

He would sit there silent for many hours, having much leisure for thought and, as the years passed, getting somewhat stouter than he had been in his first youth, but not so that he could not endure, and he had a sure rule, for men knew him to be both wise and strong, patient to hear, and ruthless when there was a good need.

Now he was troubled in mind with a great cause. It was not Bira who vexed his peace, as she often would, though he had a doubt that she was the root cause, even of this, for the gods (on whose ways he had tried ever to shape his own) are of a patient kind. Bira had tricked them once (there was little doubt of that), and though it was eighteen years ago they had been in no haste. They had shown their wrath in a slow way. They were showing it now. There was no heir to the power he held. If things went on as they now did, there need be no grief for that, for there would be no people to rule.... And now there was this tale of one who came from the gods.... Well, he would see Huni again.

Huni was one of those who had sat at the cave mouth. He was the one who sat in the midst. He was old now. He had taught Bwene in youth, but now he knew that Bwene had grown to be wiser than he. Bwene would still talk to him as he talked to none other, using plain and equal words, and showing his mind at times in a bare way.

"Huni," the King said, when they sat together in the Cave of Words, where none could come near unseen: "I would hear this tale for a second time."

"King, it is soon told, though it be very strange, so that I think at times that I walked in sleep to the Sacred Cave."

"That cannot be, or there had not been three who saw the same thing.... Did she look such a one as could be of the gods themselves, or such as they would send of a good will?"

"King, it is a hard question to tell. She did not look assured, as a god should. She looked troubled, and bewildered of mind, as one who knew not why she was there. Yet she was serene and quiet, as one who meant no evil to us, and who controlled fear. She is of a fine form, being also larger and whiter than we. There were bruises upon her, as though she had not come to earth by a quiet path, and blood had dried on a cut thigh."

"Did the Old One come out?"

"We did not see her at all. When the goddess spoke, Tela told us to go, and led her into the cave."

"That being the goddess's word?"

"I cannot say. It was a strange tongue."

"Yet Tela could understand?"

"I cannot tell that.... She would have us think that she did.... Tela hath thine own wisdom, though it may shake with a girl's fears."

The King looked wroth at that word, and yet more troubled than wroth.

"That," he said, "was foolish to say."

"It is unsaid."

"It is foolish even to think. The Old One bears her own young."

"It is the faith we hold. It is known to be so to all."

Then they paused, for Bira entered the Cave of Words. She was still in the vigour of youth, and had a face that was dark and fierce and proud, and she was very tall for her race, being nearly of the King's height.

She spoke to Huni, and there was contempt in her voice. "What is this tale I hear of a war in which all must join? Would you be the first to have your blood sucked through an ape's teeth?"

"Queen," the King interposed, "it being through you that this trouble comes, as we three know who are here, you would do better to sit still in your own place."

Bira looked at the King, and there was anger in her eyes, and a light of mockery, but no fear, though she knew well the peril in which she walked.

"Will you lay it at my door that you cannot beget a male child?"

The King started, and then checked his words. He looked at her with considering eyes. "Would you have it all said?" he asked at last, and there was silence at that, for they all looked back at the same things, though seeing them in their own ways.

The King's thoughts moved forward to a year ago when the plague came to the land. It was a plague that did not haste, causing one to sicken here, and one there, but it did not cease. It fell most on the children and the young men, causing them to lie in the caves while their strength went, so that when they died they were so thin that a man might carry three in a bundle under his arm. It had spread from end to end of the land, and had become worse in the winter days....

Bira saw other things.... She saw a light that went out. She felt that the babe was gone, and that another was between her hands. She walked back by a secret way, holding its mouth that it should not cry at a wrong time. It could cry on the next day, when it would have cause enough, but the babe was not hers, and she cared nothing for that. That had been two hours before dawn.... She saw the face of the girl Gwa. She could not speak, for the hands that were round her throat.... She saw other things. Things that she only could see, being known to none else.

Huni saw a less thing. He saw a birthmark under the arm of the priestess of the Sacred Cave. He saw the Old One reach out, and a garment pulled. He had made his eyes blank in his head at that time, and he still lived.

They saw different things, but their thoughts walked in the same way. There was no need for words, which, to Bira, might have had an ill sound. Yet she looked at the King, and her glance was level and unafraid. "A king may say what he will. Is it fault of mine that I do not breed, having borne once?"

"It is fault neither of thine nor of mine," the King answered. "It is the gods' curse."

She made no answer to that, and after a pause the King spoke again. "It is a curse that might be borne, if it were that, and no more; but our backs bleed from a worse scourge."

Bira answered then, and her contempt had but a thin veil. "It is ever the gods, when an evil falls. You call it a gods' curse that our young men sicken and die, and you would have me think that they have sent One to our aid from their own place. Which will you have it to be?"

Huni said: "Queen, that is soon said. They may have fed their wrath till their skins stretched, and they would save those who yet live."

CHAPTER EIGHT

RAINA followed her guide without fear, for the millenniums may pass, but the bases of confidence do not change. She had seen friendliness in eyes which might have been those of a girl of her own kind, except that they were a darker blue than was common among her race. Her instinct told her that this girl was of gentle moods, though she had seen her making play with a gourd of blood.

She followed without fear, but without ease, for the way was narrow, and though the floor was smooth, having been trodden for many years, the walls were rough, and the way was not straight.

The priestess, as she had been called by the old men, and of whom the King had spoken by name, calling her Tela, walked without care, having gone in and out by that way since she could first stand, nor was she quick to see what was wrong, for those dark-blue eyes were content in a dusky gloom, which was day to them, and more vexed by the glare of too bright a noon; but when she did guess she slackened pace, and then reached backward a timid hand, which was soft and slim.

So they came to a cave of the size of a large room, its extent seeming somewhat more than it was, because the roof was so low that it could be touched by a lifted hand.

To this ceiling two small covered lamps were fixed, giving a faint diffused light. Raina thought: "How can life endure in such gloom?" She could not know that it was all the light that was needed by Tela s eyes, and that more would be a glare which must be faced at times, though it was tiring to do.

Tela stopped here, saying that which meant little, except for its tone, for the words were strange. Gesture said more. In fact, she asked her guest to wait there, while she went to tell have been hard to understand, even had the words been clear, for the cave had neither chair nor stool. But Tela tried gesture again. She sat on the floor. With a gently imperative hand she drew her guest down to her side. Then she rose, with a backward motion of her hand which was clear enough. Raina sat still, watching her go out at the further end of the cave. It was not hard to sit thus, for the floor was soft with the skins of seals.

It was long before Tela returned, so that there was leisure to think, and to look round. Not having understood the conversation at the mouth of the cave, Raina had no idea that she could be regarded as an expected visitor of celestial origin, nor of the status of her whose guest she had now become. But she felt that she was in a better atmosphere than that of the ape-men of the higher plateau. She had reason to thank a very sulky and frightened bird, who now sat by a high nest refusing to explain what had occurred in an intelligent manner to a mate who was rather larger and more powerful than himself, and could lift heavier weights from the ground. She would always think that he had been trying to show off in a silly way.... But he had clone Raina a good turn, though she hadn't recognised it in time to thank him before he went....

Tela went on by other passages which were not lighted at all. She came to an inner cave where the Old One sat. The Old One had once been known as the Priestess or Witch of the Hills, but when Tela had been invested with the same sacred rank, she had become the Old One in the mouths of men.

Few had seen her in recent years, for she was reluctant to go out to the light. The fact was that she had become almost blind, which she thought that even Tela did not suspect. Tela knew it well, but she knew also that it was a thing which she was not supposed to observe.

Now the Old One sat with a graving tool in her hand. She drew pictures upon the wall of the cave. That had been her occupation for many years, which had enabled them to pass without the monotony of life becoming difficult to endure. Such pictures covered the walls of caves that went far into the hills. They had had a use at first, being like the names of streets. She had begun them after she had been lost in a dark labyrinth into which she had wandered too far. There had been three days without food before she had found the way out. Had there not been water in the inner caves, she would not have come back alive.

So she had explored more gradually after that, drawing signs, such as a man's hand or a fish's tail, where there was turning or fork, so that the way back could not be missed.

After that, she had found joy in the work itself. She had found that she could draw with bold and simple lines that brought man and beast to life. She had had much joy in that toil, though it was known to none but Tela, and she could look for no praise of men.

Now she still drew, though her sight was not clear, and her hand shook. She did not know that she was spoiling a better work of earlier years, over which the tool moved. Tela did not venture to tell her that. Why should we cause grief to the old, whom, in some measure, we love?

Tela told her tale, beginning at that which was least hard to believe.

"Huni," she said, "spoke for the King. He sought a sign that would rouse the land."

The Old One had not lost her wits, though her hand shook. She did not know whether she herself believed in the oracles which she gave, but she knew that it was wisdom to learn the minds of those who besought her aid. She supposed that Tela believed without reservation or doubt, for so she had been taught, and she was of a quiet and gentle habit of speech, which would seldom dispute. Yet she could be trusted to undertake even such interpretations as these, having wisdom in what she said. The Old One would have taken the divination herself, but it would have exposed her blindness to all. She could not face the light of the open day, and the King's counsellors could not have seen the shape that the ashes took in the dim light of the caves.

So she had trusted Tela, having no choice; but she was not herself. Quiet of manner and mood, she was yet of a cool wit. Timid of heart, and with no ambition to rule or guide, she was yet one who might do a brave thing in a frightened way. At the last test, she might show much of her father's wisdom, and something of the spirit of Bira, whose child she was.

"What," the Old One asked, "does the King seek?"

"I think he would lead us all to a new land. He would go up the river, or to the land of the Ho-Tus."

"That," the old woman answered, "would be no less than the end. This evil has made us too weak to go forth to war."

"Yet he thinks that we get worse, and the chance less."

The Old One thought by this that Tela was of the same mind as the King, which she was not quick to approve. She thought the project beyond their strength, and she had a personal fear. What would become of her, if the tribe should move? She was too ancient to leave the caves. She had not passed the entrance for fifty years: for nearly twenty she had not looked out, except by night, finding that her eyes ached. There was a new sharpness in her voice as she asked: "You have not told them the gods approve? Such signs are not easy to read. What did the bowl show?"

"It showed the form of a barren woman who came down the gorge."

"That could be read in more ways than one. What did you read it to be?"

"There was more than that. But I have not read it at all. I told them that I must refer all to you. They are to come again at the noon hour.... But there was more than that. When we looked up, the woman had come from the gods."

"You mean a real woman?"

"Yes. One who could move and speak."

"Your eyes were dazzled by the sun's light."

"No. It is something different from that. She is now in the outer cave. I left her there while I told."

"Then it is a trick of the King."

"I have thought of that. But how could he guess what the bowl would show?"

"Of what sort is she? Would she be priestess, and take your place?"

"I cannot say. She seems bewildered and strange. It would not be hard to think that she has come from the gods. She is not of our land, nor of the ape-men, nor is she black like the Ho-Tus.... She cannot speak in our tongue."

"She has come from the gods, and cannot speak in our tongue! What use is there in her...? I must see of what sort she is."

The Old One rose with a creaking of rheumatic bones, and then paused, remembering that she could see little. It would be best to ask Tela all she could first. Questions would seem queer after she had looked with her own eyes. She still thought she had to deal with a King's trick. Or it might be some strange illusion of Tela's; some vision that could not last. Probably when they got to the outer cave, the apparition would not be there. She asked: "What is she like?"

"She is taller than I. Her hair is short and dark like the winter boughs, with some sunlight within the brown. Her skin is white. I do not mean white like a cod's flesh, but she is lighter than we. She wears a piece of cloth, rough and torn, that conceals her loins."

"That is not in the way of gods."

"No. But she is bare besides that, which is not after the way of our women, nor of the Ho-Tus, who call it shame to reveal their knees.... She has a long wound on the leg, from which the blood has run down. It is a new wound of this day. Her arms have been pricked with the poison-thorn about two days ago."

"Is that all?"

"No. She had turned up the cloth she wore, at one side, making it a bag for such fruit as the ape-men eat."

"Then it was the high plateau from which she came."

"Yes. Or, at least, down the gorge. There are more than one of those trees on the side of the cliff, further up the gorge, though they do not thrive, the heat being too great for them.... Huni thought it meant that we are to attack the ape-men, and win the fruit for ourselves."

"If Huni said that, it is no less than the King's will, who must have sent the woman; therefore, I will see what she can say for herself. It may be she will talk to me."

Tela made no answer to this, being unconvinced. She thought again, how could the King have foreseen what the bowl would show? But she was accustomed to be silent when she did not agree. It is a habit which is saving of many words.

CHAPTER NINE

AT the next noon, the King himself came to the cave's mouth, which he had not done since about the time that Tela was born, for he had considered that, since the Old One would not come forth, it would reduce his dignity that he should go to her. But now he was both anxious to know what the oracle would pronounce, and curious to see this strange woman the gods had sent. But he gained little either for ears or eyes.

Tela met him at the cave mouth with the news that she who came from the gods would not be seen for two moons, after which she would both reveal herself and disclose her will. The King felt thwarted and vexed. "If it be the will of the gods that we take the fruit which the ape-men grow, we cannot be told too soon."

"If the gods' will be thus," Tela answered adroitly, "they will wish it done when the main crop is ripe, which the ape-men store for the winter days. After two moons, the right time will be very near."

"Yet," the King answered, for he was not one who was easily turned from his own will, "I would have word of hope; for the folk die."

As he said this, his thoughts were divided between the errand on which he came and the priestess to whom he spoke, who, he had little doubt, was his own child. He thought her beautiful, as she was, by the standards of any age, for beauty is not a fashion that can learn change; and he saw that in her eyes which told him that she was Bira's child; yet she was very different from her, being smaller and of less imperious ways. He had a doubt of how she would do when the Old One should die, as she soon must.... Yet, for all he knew, the Old One might be dead now. It was long since she had been seen of any at the cave mouth. Tela did all in her name.

Now she was silent for a time, and then said, in a quiet, confident tone: "You may have word of hope. There will be fewer deaths from this day."

The King was glad of that word. He was glad that it could be heard by Huni and others who stood behind. They could be trusted to spread it abroad, and men would not say that it was for nought that the King had stood at the witch's door, and had not been asked to go in. He saw, too, that Tela had said no more than a likely thing, for the deaths had grown fewer the year before as the summer waned and then worse again in the winter days.

Yes, with that word, he could tell the people to wait for two moons, giving them no more than the expectation of something great to be done after that time, when she should appear whom the gods had sent. Yet he made one more effort to gain light on what that should be when its time came. He said: "If you could show me something of the gods' will, though it were no more than as one who lifts a skirt to the knee, I might do much to prepare, which may be worse done at the last."

Tela thought again. She could not tell that which she did not know, but she felt that she must make better answer than that, speaking where many heard.

"Would you," she asked, "that the thing you are then to do should be the talk of two moons? Can you stay talk with a wall? Even now, there is too much said."

The King was silent, seeing the wisdom of what she urged. If they were to attack the Ho-Tus in two months' time, it would be ill indeed that there should be rumour spread at an earlier day. Even the ape-men might have ways by which they could learn. There were other possibilities.... He saw that it would be best to wait.... He saw also that Tela might be more fit for the place she held than he had first thought.

"Tell the Old One," he said, "that we will wait with quiet minds for the two moons, knowing that all will be well at last."

"All is well," Tela replied, "when the gods speak, for we are dust in their breath."

She went back to tell the Old One of what had passed, who was well content. The Old One played for delay. Indeed, what else could she do? She understood the King's mind. His people had become too numerous for the land they held, which, though it was fertile and flat, might not be so healthful for them as the distant hills from which their fathers had come, or the wooded country which they had occupied for a shorter time, till they had been driven out by the Ho-Tus. Where they now were, they had decreased in virility as their numbers grew. Now disease was reducing these numbers, and it is a basic instinct, both of men and animals, to seek new ground when they are afflicted thus.

But where could the tribe go, with a good hope? They could not conquer the Ho-Tus. She was sure of that. They might have a better chance against the ape-men, though they would gain less. There was little to sustain life on the high plateau. It was true that they would gain the fruit on which the ape-men fed. There might be a source of health in that change of diet, and it was natural that the minds of Huni and his companions should have been opened to such a thought when they saw the strange woman, as they looked up from the divination bowl, with the fruit in her folded skirt.

But the Old One saw that the King's plan might go beyond that. If he could gain control of the plateau, he might seek some fairer land on its further side. There must be many lands (she supposed) that were empty of men. Who had ever come to the earth's end?

Thinking of this, she saw better hope. Why should they not come to a peaceful bargain with the Ho-Tus, that they should go through their land, doing harm to none, seeking that which was farther off? That would be better than strife, even for the Ho-Tus, who, though they would surely win, would sustain some loss, and gain nothing at all.

But though she might see the wisdom of such a plan, it was one that she would be slow to speak, for she neither wished to leave the cave, nor to be left there alone.

Besides, there was the question of this strange woman, who might have come from the gods, though it was a tale that she would be slow to believe. But she must resolve that first. And it was not easy to do, till they could speak in a common tongue. The woman seemed content to stay, and of friendly mood. She responded quickly to any effort to communicate by signs, or the learning of words. Tela must be diligent both to learn and teach. When they could talk, they could learn what she was, and with what object she came. She might be from the gods indeed, in which case it would be worse than vain to oppose their will. Or she might be a useful tool. Meanwhile, Tela must speak such words that the King would be content to sit still.

44

CHAPTER TEN

RAINA found that she was expected to stay in the witch's cave, which she was very willing to do. It gave her an opportunity of learning the ways of this strange people to whom she had come, while she was quiet and safe, as she could not otherwise have expected to be. She felt that Tela was a friend. Of the Old One she was less sure, but she saw little of her. After the first interview, which was no more than a gazing upon one another in a dim light, the Old One kept to herself. She sat brooding in her own cave, or spent long hours carving on the rock, not knowing that she was sometimes defacing that which she had done better before.

Tela was more than a casual companion. It became evident from the second day that she was diligent to instruct: she did not want to learn her guest's tongue, but to teach hers. She enquired for Raina's name, which she gave, and which Tela found easy to say. But beyond her name, Tela asked nothing of her. She was intent only to teach her own tongue, which her guest was as keen to learn. Having nothing else to do, she learnt fast.

Meanwhile she knew nothing of the land or people to which she had come. But for those three men whom she had seen seated with Tela around the bowl, she would have had no evidence that there were others alive in those parts. For though she was not forcibly prevented from going abroad, and was probably of a strength to overcome both Tela and the Old One had it been put to the test, she was discouraged from the attempt. Tela's hand would be on her arm, if she moved toward the outer passage, and she would address her in pleading or warning words, which might not be understood, but their purpose was clear.

Not knowing what perils there might be for an ignorant stranger abroad, it would have been foolish to go out, having no cause, and being so warned by one who had the voice of a friend. When they could speak and exchange thoughts, she would know what it all meant, and could judge for herself. So she stayed within, learning words.

She saw signs from the first, which were more than confirmed as her knowledge grew, that these people were of a higher intelligence, and had a more complex civilisation, than that of the ape-men. As the language lessons advanced beyond the names of objects that the cave held, and the elementary actions and emotions that are common to all, Tela found difficulty in communicating ideas or facts which had no visual basis. She overcame this by drawing the things to which she would give a name, which she could do with swiftness and skill.

Her material was a rubber-like substance, which she would heat and then roll out to a thin sheet, in which condition it took the impressions of a metal stylus, smaller than, though otherwise similar to, that with which the Old One drew on the rock. While it was still warm, the marks upon it could be obliterated by a finger's pressure, but as it cooled they became indelible, unless the material should be heated again, when its surface could be smoothed anew. Raina learned that there was a great store of such sheets in the recesses of the Old One's cave. They bore ancient writings in a picture alphabet which Tela could read, but made no effort to teach, for which there might have been less than time. But it was not a thing which she would have been quick to do, had the time been much more than it was, for the knowledge of that writing was private to the Old One and herself alone. She would need to be much surer of Raina, much more certain of who or what she might be, before she would think to teach her the secret language which was for those of the Sacred Cave.

In fact, in the first days, Raina was much readier to give friendship than Tela was to respond. That was natural enough. Raina sought friends. Her instinct told her that here was one whose friendship would be of a good kind. But Tela was on her guard, being faced by a strange thing.

Yet Tela also lacked friends, though she was less aware of her need. She had been isolated from birth. What did she know, what had she seen, beyond the cave mouth, or that which the Old One taught? Well, something more of both than the Old One had ever guessed. Yet she had been held apart from her kind by the fact that she was the Old One's child (as was supposed), and the priestess-to-be....

Raina soon learnt the routines of the cave life. Every evening, as the dusk fell, Tela would go out to take food which was brought to the mouth of the cave, and at the same time she would carry out the refuse of the past day, which would be removed by those who came with the food, that there should be no pollution around the cave.

After the bringing of food, there would be no man in the river gorge, which would be sacred from that hour to those who dwelt in the cave. It was then, in the moonlight nights, that Tela would go out to bathe in the stream.

As the days passed, and friendship grew, Tela took Raina with her at these times, and, as confidence came, Tela told at last how she had wandered at night, even from childhood, while the Old One slept. She had not (as she thought) ever been seen, for the folk did not stir abroad without a great cause when the moon shone, believing that sickness came from its light. That was what the Old One taught, it having come down to her from the wisdom of ancient days. Raina wondered whether it might have originated in the fertile mind of some young priestess who, like Tela, wished to walk in the night.

It was by knowledge gained in these moonlight wanderings, rather than through the Old One's teaching, that Tela was able to explain so much of the life of the tribe from which she was held apart.

Raina responded, as their ability of conversation grew, by telling what she could of the civilisation from which she came, and Tela, listening, saw that she was a goddess indeed.

She told also of how the ape-men had tried to enslave her, and how she had made use of the great bird to descend into the gorge. Raina did not aim to give an untrue account, but her choice of words was not great. As Tela saw it, it became a miraculous thing. Raina, looking with contempt on the puny efforts of the ape-men to confine her against her will, had descended on a bird's back. She was a goddess indeed.

This revelation made Tela shy for a time, but the friendship between the two was a thing too natural for such a barrier to hold it back. Tela reflected that she was a priestess herself, which, if not quite equal to being a goddess, comes rather near. She believed (as did all the tribe) that she had the power to produce a female child by her own will, which, when the Old One died, it would become her duty to do. There were writings which the Old One did not allow her to read as yet, which would tell her how this could be done. Tela thought vaguely of ceremonies and incantations.

If the Old One should die, having told her no more, it would be her first duty to read these secret records (which she would then be the only one living who would be able to do), and she would know more than she did now....

In the light of a full moon which rose to a cloudless sky, Tela led her friend down the path of the gorge, with the cliff wall rising on their left hand, and the shining instability of the river breaking up the moonlight upon their right. She led on to where the gorge opened, as the high cliffs ceased, and they heard the distant sound of the ocean breaking upon a beach that was less than two miles away.

The air was cooler here, under the starlit sky, than it had been in the gorge. A wind blew from the north which they had not felt before. Raina looked round in expectation of unfamiliar things, but there was nothing before her but the sand dunes, and the river flowing down to the sea.

She would have gone forward, following the river's course, but Tela touched her with a timidly restraining hand, and they turned southwards, keeping under the shadow of the high cliff.

Even here, Tela paused. She seemed afraid to speak, and uncertain whether to go on. Under her breath she said: "Too much light." She would have preferred clouds to this glare of a moon at full, and the starlit sky. But they went forward silently, taking what shadow they could, and as they went the land became fertile and broad, and the sound of the tide grew fainter and then ceased.

When they had passed the mouths of caves in the high cliffs, which were like to the one from which they came, and which were for the King's use and those of his own household, Tela moved with less caution, only watching, as they came near the dwellings of men, that they kept to the shadows, lest they should be visible to any who looked out through the latticed squares through which light and air entered the Baradi huts.

Raina noticed that in every hut a lamp burned, making it at once less likely that they would be seen by those who dwelt within, and easy for them to observe the sleepers, if they ventured to look through the lattice bars. Tela had done that many times before, and had learned some things of the ways of the tribe which she would not otherwise have done. She would have learnt more, but for the fact that it was not easy to look downward through the lattices from without. It was easier to see roof and walls than the floor on which the folk slept.

"Why," Raina asked, "do they burn lights through the night?"

"It is to keep out the dark, which is bad to breathe, though it does no harm to us, who are of the priestly race."

"That," Raina said, "has a foolish sound."

"Folly," Tela agreed, "is always easy to find."

Raina would have added that darkness cannot be breathed, being nothing more than the absence of light, but she was short of words, and had learned already that it was better to be still than to attempt that which might be beyond her power to express.

She turned her thoughts to the moonlit gardens and fields, which, in that softened light, seemed to be well cultivated and well kept, and not unbelievably different from those of the fairer land from which she had come. But there were few trees, and there was no luxuriance in the growth of crops on the level land.

"How many are there," she asked, "of the men of your tribe?"

This was not answered with ease, but Tela, using patience and craft of words, made herself understood in the end. There had been seventeen thousand, fit for labour or war, two years ago, but that number was not more than twelve now, of whom four thousand were seal-hunters and catchers of fish, who might be hard to move inland. These men had large flat-bottomed boats, or rafts, on which they would migrate for several months of each year to islands where they could catch seals. When they came home, they spent their time fishing in nearer seas.

"We have lost already one strong man out of three, and they still die," Tela said, "but that is not all, nor, perhaps, the worst. The boy children have died so fast that our young men must be fewer each year. For twenty years, they will be less with the passing of every year, even though there should not be another death from today. That is why the King would have the tribe moved while its strength is no less than now."

Raina knew by this time of the peril in which the people lay, and of the part which she was expected to take. She understood that she was believed to have been sent by the gods, which she did not deny. She saw that it might even have a kernel of truth. What is sure, in a world in which all is strange? Only those who are dull of mind can be slow to wonder and doubt, and the more we learn the fewer certainties we may have.

But as Tela explained these things, and learned what she could of Raina's own world, her own doubt grew. She did not doubt that Raina came from a higher race. She would have called her goddess with ready will. But she saw that, if she had been sent to aid the land, she had not known that for which she came.

Yet she might help none the less—if Tela knew what she would have her to do, of which she was not sure. And, in any case, that was for the Old One to say.

Meanwhile, as the weeks passed, affection and confidence grew between two who were girls together, though we may call them goddess or priestess, or what we will. And the day was near when the King would send again to ask that the oracle be interpreted, and the will of the gods revealed. Tela looked for the Old One to speak, which she did not do She had ceased to draw. She ate little. She sat on the floor of her dark cave, with eyes fixed on the ground. Often, she did not answer when Tela spoke.

"It is the noon after next that the King will send Huni here, unless he shall come himself once again," Tela said. "I must ask my mother to say what the oracle meant, or I must resolve it in my own way. It is not a thing to be left unthought till the last hour."

She spoke timidly, as one diffident and perplexed, and yet Raina thought, as King Bwene had thought before, that she might do better at a hard pass than would many who faced the world with a bolder front. The next morning she spoke again in the same way. "I will ask my mother now," she said, "for her speaking cannot be longer delayed."

She went, leaving Raina in the outer cave, as she had done at the first. But she learned nothing of what the Old One may have pondered in those silent days, for she had sunk sideways on to the floor from the place where she had been seated, being quite dead.

CHAPTER ELEVEN

TELA raised a form which was strangely light. She had never before lifted her whom she called mother, and who had been her sole guardian and companion from the first weeks of her life. There had, in fact, been little closeness of physical intimacy between them, and their souls had been far apart.

The Old One, even in younger days, had not been of those who will give confidence to a child, and to her wisdom or admonitions Tela had listened with little argument or dispute, even with little questioning after the first years, receiving all that she heard in a quiet way, that gave little sign of her own thoughts. Yet the Old One would have been surprised to know how well she was understood.

She laid the shrivelled form on a pile of sealskins in a low corner of the cave, which had been its bed when alive. She went back to Raina. She said: "My mother is dead." It was spoken without tears, but there was that in the tone which expressed a world of desolation within her heart. Yet it was less than would have been had Raina not come to the cave, and had she been more absolutely alone.

She remembered that the oracle must be expounded on the next day. There would be no help from the Old One now. She must do it herself. Unless Raina would. She had no jealousy of Raina, not being one who desired to rule. Yet it was not her way to refuse to do the part which became hers. Raina said: "I will give you any help that I can."

Tela felt better for that promise, though she would have preferred that Raina should have taken control, and that she should have been the one to give help. But she saw that that could not be. Raina was even more ignorant than herself of the conditions of the problem which must be faced, and of the ways of her tribe. Tela must decide for herself what should be said to the King at tomorrow's noon. But Raina would give her all the help that she could....

There was another matter on her mind, rivalling, if not exceeding, in urgency that of the oracle which she must pronounce tomorrow. There were the writings to which she had had no access till now: those that were to be read at once when her mother died. Those that held strange knowledge by which each priestess in turn must guide her life, and by which their line continued its generations. Even Raina must know nothing of them.

Raina asked: "Should you not let it be known that your mother is dead?" She remembered that there might be none who would come till the sunset neared, when food would be brought to the cave.

"I cannot tell," Tela answered, "what I shall do, till I have read that which my mother wrote. I have her charge to do nothing at all before that."

She went back to her mother's cave, and to the recess which was near her bed. She took out many tablets which she laid aside, being those which she knew. She found a pile beyond them which had changed colour somewhat from age, but the writings were still clear. There were some also more recent which were in her mother's hand, but which she had not seen before then.

She sat down on the cave floor to read these, thinking that she would be alone while she learned things which were strange and new, and which she supposed that she must not speak. Even from Raina, she was a priestess apart.

She felt this the more as she read the first tablet of instructions which the Old One had written, for it impressed upon her the need of secrecy in all that she did. She must take no one into her confidence, until her daughter should be of an age to assist her in the rites and oracles by which they lived. These words had been written before Raina had come to the cave, but they were clear that there must be no exception at all. "Not even," the tablet warned, "to the father of your child must you tell aught."

What might be the meaning of that? Puzzled brows drew together over the dark-blue eyes. Well, she must read more. Doubtless, she would understand in the end....

But these very admonitions of secrecy, while they emphasised the importance of withholding from Raina a closer confidence, increased the sense of isolation which depressed her mind. Twice she rose with the thought that she would take as many of the secret tablets as she could bear, and decipher them in the outer cave where Raina was. Twice she sat back, feeling that she should be alone while she read that which was only meant for her own eyes. But she rose a third time with the thought that it could make no difference, if she did not tell what she read, that Raina should be near, she not being skilled to read. So she took as many tablets as she could, and went where Raina was, sitting down at her side. She read long, and Raina could see at times that she was puzzled, and at times excited or troubled, by that which she read; but she said nothing, leaving Tela to speak if she would.

Tela was grateful for that. After a time she ceased to read, and sat long with her thoughts. She said, half aloud: "The Old One was very wise." It sounded as though she would still a doubt in her own mind.

Raina spoke at last: "Is there any help I can give?"

"My mother," Tela answered, "is not to be seen of men. You can help me in that." But she did not answer as one whose trouble would be met by such help, but rather as one who had been disturbed from a different thought.

After that, they took the Old One by a long path into a distant cave where there was a pool, very black and deep. Tela carried the body, wrapped in a cloak of skins, and Raina bore a light, of which Tela had the less need. When they came there, they sank the body with stones that the cave supplied, Tela using certain rites which the tablet had enjoined her to do, about which we need not pause, for they are nothing to us.

CHAPTER TWELVE

TELA looked at Raina and her lips opened and closed. She was not the first, by several, who had read those tablets and been led in an hour's space into a world of thought where all was strange, and values altered or fell. But those others had been alone with their thoughts through the slow hours, that might have drawn into months before they had become the settled furniture of their minds, or would be the roots from which action grew.

If Tela must not tell, might she not ask? There were things, she felt, that Raina could tell which might resolve much. She felt that Raina had a far wider knowledge and a different experience of life than were hers at that time. A minute's speech might save her a week of thought. Yet she was not one who was likely to be betrayed by any rashness of words. What is said in a minute's space may be regretted for more weeks than one. She had learned that when she was younger than now.

Besides that, her mind was a chaos of many thoughts which would not lie quiet, nor could she consider any for long, for they would be smothered by others that were thrown up volcanically, to be overwhelmed in their turn.

She was not a child of the Old One.... She was Bira's child.... It was all tricks and cheats.... The tablets did not say that, but every word was pregnant with that assumption.... She was Bwene's child. The only child of the King.... An oracle should always be so worded that it could be read in two ways so that you could not be proved to be wrong when the event came.... She had no mysterious creative power. She must steal a girl-child by some sleight, and with a cunning that no one would ever guess; or she must find a father for one that she must bear alone in the dark caves.... A child that must be a girl, or it must not live, and it must be done all over again.... It was a folly to foretell life or death, or, indeed, anything definite that would bring her to disrepute if it should befall in a diverse way. But if you should be caught in that trap, you must bring it to pass. If you should say that a man would die, die he must, though it be by your secret hand.... There were many ways by which a priestess might become a mother with no risk that it would be told among men. There were accounts of how it had been done in earlier days, and in different ways. There had been one at the first that had been secret and sure. The priestess who lacked an heir would seek the man she chose in the night. She would whisper that it was a goddess who came, whose presence would blind him should she be seen. Hence she could only come when the moon was down. When she had had what she would, she would still him with strong drugs, or a dagger's point.

That method had worked well, and for more times than a few, till (how do such things become known?) there had come a proverb that he must die whom a goddess kissed in the dark. After that, there had grown up a tale that the dark itself was an evil to be kept out of a healthy hut. That tale might come from a different source, but it had the same effect as though it had been designed.... But these things must be put aside now, for the King would be here at the next noon, and what should be said to him?

"Raina," Tela asked, "will you tell me all that you can about the ape-men on the level height? Are they many or few?"

Raina could give little answer to that, but she told what she could. They pooled knowledge. The ape-men did not seem very formidable. Perhaps the fruit that their gorges bore would really bring the health which the tribe lacked. Perhaps that had really been the meaning of the way by which Raina had come, and the fruit she held. It was the idea in the King's mind. It pointed to an enterprise which might be within the present strength of the tribe. It did not involve that Tela should leave the caves which had been her home from birth, and in which she dwelt as a priestess apart. To do that would be an adventure from which she shrank, though it had some allure too.... Besides, there was a way she could help in such a war, of which the King himself did not know...

When the King came at the noon of the next day, Tela met him at the cave mouth, and there was no doubt in her mind as to what she should say.

Raina stood at her side. She wore no more than such a kirtle as that in which she had first appeared to those who had been grouped round the bowl of blood, though it was not now made from a sack which was soiled and torn. Tela had seen to that. It was now of the finest cloth which the tribe wove, and stained with a dark blue which was almost black. Tela had said: "You can have white if you choose, but it will soon soil, when you go abroad, as I suppose you must when the tribe moves. There are other dyes, but they are in common use, both by women and men. You should have that which will place you apart." She did not offer the scarlet which she wore herself, and which was sacred to her. Perhaps that would have been more than she could have been expected to do. Nor would it have suited Raina, as it did her.

Raina would have worn more, if she might, but against that Tela had been firm. "It is the way of gods to go bare, as you now do, and as you were when you came. It is not the way of women of mortal kind. Had you come clothed as ourselves, you might have been taught the feel of a master's whip, if you had come to no worse ending than that."

That she talked thus (though she did it without thought of offence) showed that she had lost the fear that it was a goddess to whom she spoke. That was of instinct rather than reason, for she still had a great doubt in her mind as to what Raina might be. But she felt that they were comrades for the days that were now at hand, and it was essential to her, as to Raina herself, and to the good of the tribe, that she should be a goddess revealed to men.

So they came out side by side to give audience to the King at the cave's mouth. The King did not come alone. Huni was there, and a dozen others who were leaders of men, whom the King would have to hear what the oracle would pronounce. He did not think that the Old One would fail him now. Anyway, it was best that it should be heard of all.

There were no women there, for that would have been against the customs that ruled the land.

The King looked at Tela with friendly eyes, but he had seen her when last he came, and now he turned to a stranger sight—to one who was whiter and taller than the women of his own race, and who walked unashamed in a bold way, being more than the daughters of men.

Raina looked on a king who had left his youth, and whose girth was more than it once had been, though he was still active and strong. He had the manner of one who ruled, and his eyes were those of a man who thought much. Raina thought him the best man she had yet seen in this savage land, as, indeed, he was. He looked at Raina, and he felt more than he thought or saw. Their glances met, and his fell.

It was to Tela he spoke, while she looked at him with new eyes, knowing now that he was father as well as king. She wondered, did he know that? Perhaps he did. He had the look of one who knew much. But it was a thing that must not be said: that was best unthought.... Her mind adjusted itself to the moment's need, as she heard his words: "Priestess," he said, "it is the hour at which you will show us the gods' will."

"The gods say: 'They shall go up when the moon is full'."

"That will be ten nights from now."

"It will be the tenth night."

"Do the gods promise that we prevail? Do the gods bless?"

"They bless those who are first to go, but there is a curse on the lagging feet. He who is last will lie soon in a narrow bed."

The King heard, and was well content. There was no need to ask where it was meant that they should go. There was but one upward way from that land. To go up, at whatever point, was to come to the high plain where the ape-men dwelt. Yet he saw that there must be more said. He did not know what part Raina should have in this, but he saw that it was a vital thing that she should be there to inspire the tribe.

"Is this," he asked, "what the bowl showed? Or has the Old One had later word from the gods themselves?"

"The Old One," Tela answered, "is here no more. She has gone to the gods herself, and I am priestess alone from this hour. There is more to be said, but it is not for the birds to hear.... Will you come into the cave?"

The King was glad to hear this. It was what he had wished, but had paused to ask, lest he should be refused in the hearing of those he led. He looked on them in doubt, knowing that they would be glad to come too. He did not warn them, but he thought it foolish to show his mind. Refusal should come from her.

Tela read his mind in a quick way. "Huni can come with you," she said.

The others understood from that that they must remain where they were, or could go home if they would. They sat down to wait.

CHAPTER THIRTEEN

TELA led the way to the large low cave to which she had brought Raina when first she came. Having designed to lead the King in, she had a lamp in readiness, so that he could walk at ease on that gloomy path.

They sat on the rug-strewn floor, Tela and Raina being side by side, and the King facing them, with Huni somewhat behind on his left side. Huni said nothing at this time, and may have had leisure to think the more. His time would come when the King should call him to counsel in the Cave of Words, where there would be none but they two.

"I know well," the King said, "that it must be as the gods have willed, and as has been said now in a public way. Also, I see that, if we are to go up in the night, it must be when the moon is full. Yet, had the choice been mine, I would have taken a nearer day, and I would have moved at the dawn hour. My people know that the darkness is ill to breathe."

Tela was not quick to answer this. She felt more nervous now than she had done when she had spoken to all that came. She had spoken then as one who was no more than a messenger of the distant gods. It was for those who heard to obey, not to argue on what she said. But in her heart she knew that the words were hers, and that she had sought to give counsel which would be wise in itself, and would accord with the King's will. Yet what did she know of the arraying of men, or of the needs of the war which her words would wake? Now she saw that the King was less than pleased, and her heart shook. Had she spoken that which would send her people to death?

Yet she knew that she must show neither doubt nor fear with Huni, of whom she knew little, sitting watchful behind the King. Also, she had something to show on her side which the King could not guess, but which was likely to please him well. And she had talked long with Raina, making what they had thought to be no less than a good plan.

"The moon," she said, "being full, will not set till the dawn is near.

The King pondered this. "Is it the will of the gods that we do not move till the dawn hour?"

"I speak not now from the gods, but of the moons, which know well."

The King looked at Raina, though it was to Tela that he still spoke. He was not sure that Raina could speak his tongue. "Will she whom the gods have sent be our guide on this upward way?"

"She will appear when the height is won."

The King pondered again. He looked at Raina, who had an aspect of flesh and blood—of one who might be harmed by a straight-cast spear. It might hearten his people more if she were to lead their advancing ranks, but he saw that if she should fall it would be a disaster that it would be hard to survive. Also, that she should appear on the height which she had not climbed had the sound of a god-like way. He saw beyond that, that if the ape-men should make no guess of the plans they made, the high cliffs might be scaled before resistance should show its head. Yes, from any angle it might be the best way. Anyway, it was that which the gods had willed.

He had another doubt in his mind. "It is a good word," he said, "that the gods will have no blessing for lagging feet, yet it will make it a harder thing to set out ranks in array. War is not a game in which men jostle to see who may be first; or, at least, cannot be so designed when we marshal ranks to advance. Now it seems that whoever will hold the rear, as some must, will be looked on as a cursed man."

"Yet," Tela answered to that, for it was a thing planned between Raina and her, "they will not know who is last, for the attack can be made from different points, and those who haste may be well ahead, even to him who brings up the rear. It is of that I would speak. Will you send a strong force up by this gorge when the hour comes, with two leaders whom you can most trust?"

"With how strong a force?"

"You will know better than I."

"I might, if I should know how it is meant to be used."

"That is not to be known till the hour comes."

The King looked at Raina, who gave no sign, for it was agreed that Tela should talk at this time. He remembered that she had come down the gorge. Now she was to appear on the height. He thought she knew of some place at which the gorge could be scaled. It sounded a good plan. But, in fact, it was more than that. He said: "I will send you a thousand men."

"Will you send two?"

"You must see that they cannot move more than two abreast on this way."

"Yet I would have it two thousand men."

"It was but now that you said I should be the better judge of that count."

"Yes. So you are.... You will send two leaders of skill?"

"I will send you the best I may." The King knew that such leaders must be chosen by little more than a random guess. It was long since his tribe had been arrayed on a front of war.

"And with two thousand men of your best?"

The King saw she would have her way. "Yes," he said, "it shall be the number you will.... Do you stay here yourself when the strife joins?"

The King did not urge, he sought only to know. It was tradition that the priestess must be seen in the ranks of war, for she was one whom the gods would guard, and their favour might be a cloak that would be common to all. Yet he would not that she should take a risk that he could not measure with a sure mind. She was his daughter, as they both knew, and the only priestess they had. Should she come to a quick end, it would be evil indeed.

"I cannot come," she said, "nor do I sit still when the tribe moves. I must give aid in another way." Seeing that he was about to question again, she added: "There is no more to be said at this time."

The King was silenced by that, but he was well content in his secret heart, even though Huni heard. He would have his daughter assert her power now that the Old One was dead, and seeing her so young, and of quiet ways, he had had a doubt that he was glad to lose.... His eyes went to Raina again. Did the gods send them a woman of mortal kind? Was she such that a King could wed? Or was there impiety, perhaps madness, in such a thought?

He resolved that he must put such doubts aside till the time of war should be past. After that—well she might go back to the gods, if she came from them. But if she stayed among men, she might be glad to wed with a king, for how could she do better than that?

Raina was looking at him with friendly eyes. Could she read the thoughts in his heart? If she did, would they anger her, to the ruin of all? Once again, his eyes fell before her, which was a new thing for him to know, who had ever looked where he would.

Raina thought again that he was the best man she had seen of this race, which might have been higher praise had she beheld more. She had seen the group of those who had stood behind him an hour ago, among whom there were few of less age than himself. She thought him to be one who had much care in his life, and less joy, king though he might be. But she did not guess his own thoughts, which he hid well, as a king is practised to do.

Chapter Fourteen

IT is hard to hold back that on which the mind dwells, so that it will not come to the tongue, and most so when there are two alone, except only themselves, and they friendly enough, and allied in a common plan.

Tela considered much about the new things she had read, of which few were easy to like, and there were matters there on which she would have been glad to change thoughts with another mind.

She had doubted much in the silence of younger years, and now it seemed that every doubt had been grounded well, and that she had only erred when she had believed. She had a timid strength of her own, which could bear much, though it might seem that her shoulders bent, and she had learned for long years to think what she did not say. But now her world shook.

It may be said that it was not a world of much worth, being so founded on fraud and trick, but it was all she had, and its fall could be no pleasure to her.

Other priestesses must have come to the same pass, and learned the truth in the same way, and sustained their parts to the end; but that was no help to her, for their values may not have been those which she would have priced high. They may have loved power, and other things of which a priestess would have more than a common wife, to a greater height than she did, and of those matters of which she thought they may have cared less.

Also, they may have been held by fear, for if they should have gone forth and said that their practice was falsely born, they might have been paid in an evil way.

Tela had no will to tell Raina that chain of frauds that the tablets showed, nor of their counsels for new deceits, but the doubts they brought were behind all that she thought or said, and came out at times, as they were very certain to do.

They came forward the more because Raina did not ever urge her to talk beyond her desire, letting her thoughts run in the channel themselves would choose.

It was the day after the King had heard the oracle which they had contrived together with all the wisdom they had, that Tela asked, as they sat at the cave mouth, in the darkening hour when they knew that none would approach:

"Would you say, when we divine as we do, that it is but of our own thoughts that our words are born, or are we controlled of the higher gods, even though we may not be aware of the source of that which we consider to say?" Raina had no certain answer to that, or not one which she could put into the common language they had. She said:

"When we speak of what we do with our own powers, we may give birth to less than a clear thought, for we know not what is ourselves, whom we have not made."

Tela pondered that, and saw sense. She said: "Yet I shall be in fear till I die, lest I mislead with an evil word, such as might send many to death."

"Then," Raina replied, "as I think, you will fret beyond cause, if you have said the best that you could. For you did not place yourself here, nor did you limit the wisdom you have by your own will."

"I did not place myself here, yet it must be by my own will that I so act that men will heed what I say, thinking a god speaks.... I should be more content were it all as they think it to be—which it is not, as we both know."

"As to that," Raina replied, "I can understand how you feel. I might feel alike. Yet there may be more of truth and less fraud in that which you speak and do than you can see for yourself. It must be founded on more than lies, or it could not stand as it does. For it is only where the foundations are soundly laid that you can build to a height which may be either strong or no more than a painted front of pretence. But if the foundations themselves be of rotten wood, you can build nothing thereon, good or bad, but it will sink to the ground."

"I suppose you right, for that too has a likely sound. Yet I am one to hate lies, which may be strange in itself, seeing how I was born, and of what blood."

She checked herself at that word, having had no mind to tell Raina that she was the King's child, which was too secret a thing, but Raina thought it was the Old One of whom she spoke, who would do equally well.

"We are not," she said, "as I think, of our parents, except for the instincts our bodies bring with a mother's blood. We are ourselves what we have been, and shall ever be.... That there are strange powers which are known to few, but not most, I should be foolish to doubt, for I have seen their fruits in my own land. Yet such knowledge, though being good in itself, yet being occult to most, may be used for discordant ends, as a good basket may be loaded with dirt."

Tela did not reply, being fearful lest she should be led to say more than she would. She thought of the counsel she had given, which would be repeated from mouth to mouth as though it came from the gods, and she knew (but she must not say) that she was not a priestess born by miraculous art, but the King's child, and one who had no commune with any gods. She was in a net which had not been woven by her, and which would not be easy to break in a wise way.

Raina spoke again, answering Tela's thought, as though it had been spoken aloud.

"You are vexed because you did not speak from the gods (which you cannot tell), but what harm can there be arising therefrom? You have but heartened a plan which the King had at the first. You have but pointed a road they were bound to go. You have given courage and hope. Being so boldly assured, they may succeed by that word where they would have otherwise failed, and you will have saved a people who trust in you."

Tela looked pleased at that thought, and then she asked, in a sudden way: "If they win the land where the apes dwell, do you think it will do them much good?"

"I cannot answer that, knowing no more than I do. It will give them a new land, and a new food. If it checks the disease which they cannot cure—"

Tela did not look hopeful of that. She asked: "You have seen the land. Should you call it good?"

"It is different from this low land of the coast. I cannot say more for it than that."

"Which is not much. Do you think the ape-men will be very strong?"

"I think they are fierce, and will fight hard. I should dislike their teeth in my neck, having seen how they spring and bite. I know nothing of how many they are."

"No one does. But they are not few. There is a tale that our fathers sought to make way to the higher ground when they first came to this land, and the apes gathered in a great host, slaughtering all who climbed."

"You think the land is not worth the cost it will be to win?"

"I will tell you," Tela replied, "my most secret thought, which shall be spoken to none, unless the King should be here alone, when I would say it to him. I think that we shall give the apes a hard time, being resolved as we are, but if we take the whole land for a prey, we shall not have done much. There must be something done beyond that. But it is a word which, at this day, the men would lack heart to hear. When they are glad with success, they must be pointed forward again, though the half die."

Raina listened to this, and was not the first to think that she who spoke had a courageous will hidden under her gentle and timid ways, and that she was one who would see the truth, though her heart shrank. She said: "Well, it is a matter to weigh when the fight is won. For if it be lost, it will not be needful for it to vex our minds, which will be busy with other things. But I do not think they will fail, having had comfort from you, and being desperate men—and the plan we have made ourselves should give them a great help."

Tela said: "You may be right there, and, be we priestess or goddess, or what you will, we shall know it in ten days' time, neither more nor less."

With that word she threw the shadow from off her mind, as she was able to do with the youth and health which were hers, and they rose to bathe together in the solitary river.

Even in the dusk which, to Raina's eyes, reduced all her surroundings to a shadowed obscurity, Tela could see well. She saw the stain of the brand between Raina's shoulder blades, still yellow on the whiter skin, as she had often seen it before. She had not asked concerning it, less from initial timidity than presumption that it was a permanent natural colouring. But, since then, she had watched it fade, which suggested that it might be of a different character.

Now, in the intimacy which comes to those who talk together of the larger issues of life, she found courage and curiosity to ask what it might be; and when Raina told without reserve, and with some satisfaction in the knowledge that it was likely to be less than a permanent disfigurement, Tela listened with no lack of sympathy, but with a thought that Raina might be somewhat less goddess even than she had thought her before, however distant might be the land from which she had wandered there, and however wonderful might be its habits of life, and the knowledge it had acquired.

There were wonders and wisdoms she had been told which she did not doubt, having resolved that Raina was not one to lie in a boastful way, but there was a disconcerting feature connected with them, which reduced both their importance and their reality.

Raina would tell of some invention, some contrivance or tool, which was in use in her own land, and Tela would call it good, and say: "Can we make one for ourselves?"

Or, "How would you do that?" And Raina would think awhile, and reply: "I don't quite see how we could. We should need...."

Or: "I am afraid I should be useless for that. I know it is done. But not how."

To Tela, this inability not only left the strange methods and inventions of which Raina told in a land which had the vagueness of dreams, it suggested, even beyond the truth, that she must have been an unimportant, even an inferior member of the community from which she had come.

To Raina, it brought a sharp realisation of how little separate capacity she had for the control of the complexities of the civilisation from which she came; of how little, indeed, any one individual could have.

It was a disability of which she had not been conscious before, but now she was forced to learn how little of the diffused knowledge she had was of such a nature, or sufficiently complete, to be controlled to her single use. She discovered that she knew little, though she might know about much.... As most, whether men or women, of any highly organised civilisation if they had been so placed, would have been likely to do.

CHAPTER FIFTEEN

ON the eighth day, the King came. He had sent Huni with a request that Tela would receive him within the cave, and by so doing had spared her the trouble of making the same proposal to him. She asked that he should come alone, and near to the falling of dusk, that being the time of day at which she could sit with most comfort at the mouth of the cave, as she must do if she were to know when he would arrive, and be ready to guide him in.

She said to Huni: "He must come alone for this time. Even you shall not be at his side. What I have to say, he may tell after to you, or to whom he will. That is for him to decide. But I must speak first to his own ear, for plans of war cannot be hid too closely apart."

Huni made no trouble of that. He was busy with many cares, and he knew that the King would tell him soon enough, and all he needed to know.

So the King came as the dusk neared, but he was not wholly alone. He had two with him, who were younger men than Raina had seen before.

"These," he said, "are they who will lead the two thousand men for whom you have asked that they shall be at your order here. Shall they enter, or not? For there are things of which they should be informed before then."

Raina, who was at Tela's side, saw two men who were as tall as the King, though they may have been of less weight. They were straightly and finely made, and one of them was handsome in a bold way, looking, even at her, with a fearless, insolent gaze, so that she became aware that her clothes were few, of which she had ceased to think until then.

His name was Swashki, and he was known as Swashki of the Three Wives. That was because it had been his boast, from his boyhood days, that he would have that number of wives, neither more nor less, at which men had laughed. For it had not been the custom to have more wives than one, though there had been no contrary law, and it could be done if the women would so consent, and would live in peace.

But he got the three wives he would, for he was the kind who could have his way with most women, or at least most of such as would be attractive to him: and now, when the men died so fast that he might have had a dozen more if he would (as some did), and when to have a second had become almost common throughout the land, he still had but three, saying that they were enough, and he would not change.

The other, whose name was Plini, might have seemed to some to be the better man of the two, but he was quieter of glance and mood, and his left eye was no more than a hole in his head, making his beauty less.

Tela said: "We must talk alone. Let the men wait." And she led the King to the inner cave, holding a light for his feet and Raina go-ing ahead, for, by this time, it had become a way that she knew well.

They sat down on the sealskin floor, and Bwene looked at the girl who had become priestess, by the Old One's death, while she was still young. He could not put the thought out of his mind that she was his own child, and with it a fear lest she might not be equal as yet, being so young and quiet, to the place which had become hers.

"It was an ill time," he said, "for the Old One to die, when this shadow was on the land. Have you no lack, being alone?"

She saw that he asked more than his words held, and she replied in the same way: "The Old One had taught me much, and she has left writings of weight, which I have read, as I only could do. I know much that I may not speak."

Their eyes met, and the King felt that she knew all that was in his own heart, and perhaps other things which he might not guess, and he knew well that they should not be spoken aloud, even if Raina had not been there. For a fact may be known to many, and yet have no power, whether for evil or good, if it be not spoken aloud. It will be no more than a wandering ghost, which has found no body in which to dwell. But if it be born in the spoken word, it will pass from mouth to mouth, growing ever in stature and bulk, till it have a power which those who fed it may be unequal to rule.

The King turned his words a new way, asking: "Will you tell me now what you would do with this number of men whom you have asked to have here? I must suppose that you have knowledge of some point up the canyon's course where the height can be scaled, but I have a doubt whether you are aware of how long a line will be made by two thousand men, moving not more than two abreast, as they must do at times, where the river is close to the mountain wall; nor yet of how long they will take to deploy, if they must climb by a narrow path. I talk of this so that, if they are to be used in such ways, they may start while the night is young."

"They are to be used," Tela replied, "much as you think, but not quite, nor are they all to go by one way."

"I must tell you first," she went on, "that there is a way through these caves by which the higher land may be won. I was told this by the Old Ones some years ago, but she did not show me the way. Since she has died, I have read of it on the tablets by which our wisdom is kept alive. It is not a way that could be found without one to guide, either to go or come, but it is sure, though, as I suppose, we may find it to be blocked at the higher end, so that it will be a work of spades to get free. I thought to take a thousand men by that way, each holding the hands of those who are behind and before, so that they will not fail for the dark, or a twisting path. I must go first, it being a path I will tell to none. There shall be no road through the Sacred Cave. If any should try it without a guide, they will surely die in the hollow hills, for the caves are many, and go far under the land."

The King was more pleased than surprised when he heard this, for he had known before that the caves went far inward and upward among the hills, the higher land being split many times, and by more canyons than were open to feel the sun.

"That," he said, "has a good sound. But there are another thousand for whom you asked, and you also said that the goddess"—he looked at Raina—"who can now speak with our tongue, would meet us upon the height. How do you think to contrive this?"

"It is her own plan," Tela replied. "It is good to me, but she should tell it better than I."

Raina found that she must tell her plan to the King, using the best words that she had. He listened with care, though he gave as much heed to the one who spoke as to the matter which filled her mouth. He thought the strange accent was very pleasant to hear.

"There is a place," she said, "as you come down the gorge, where the river spreads to a fair width, and there is also a wide space on the left bank, the cliff receding, and rising with less abruptness than it does elsewhere, either above or below."

"So there is. I know it well. But it is useless to us. For wherever the descent of the cliff is less than sheer, it is covered with a growth of those poisonous thorns, from which all who climbed would die

69

before they should reach the top. There is not a foot which is not sheer, but there the thorns root."

"But they do not root where the wall is sheer. Should you not say that, where they are seen, the cliff could be climbed if they were not there?"

"We may suppose that."

"And there is a place where it is covered with these thorns, even from the base to the far summit on high."

"What help is there in that?"

"The thorn is brittle and dry. Have you thought of fire?"

Bwene pondered this. "Goddess," he said, "you plan well. Yet there can be no surprise at that point, for the fire will be seen. The thorns will burn with a fierce flame, and with a smoke which is yellow and dense. It will rise over the high top of the cliff wall and be seen far, whether by night or day."

"Yet without surprise it may serve to draw them off from the main attack. It might be of use for that, though none should climb, and much more if we can ascend, under cover of smoke, before they can be there in a great force. How far will they be apart?"

Bwene pondered this. It would be further round the foot of the cliffs, but overhead he supposed that the place of thorns would be about twelve miles from the point of the shore attack. And that of the secret ascent through the hollow caves would, as they could loosely judge, be halfway between.

"Goddess," the King asked, "do you know war?"

"I know it by name, and as that which I do not love. I am not one who has a will to fight with my own hands."

"Then do you think to go up by that way when the thorns are burnt? You have a life you should guard well."

The King looked at Raina as he said this, as though to judge how her body would react to the thrust of a wooden spear. It seemed to him that she was mortal enough for the skin to break, and the blood come. He thought also that she might be mortal enough for other use, of a better kind.

Raina felt that all the time he had talked he had looked at her more than he need. She felt, as she had done under Swashki's eyes, that she wished she were better clad. She felt that, though it might be a goddess for which he looked, it was a woman he saw; and though there was more respect in his eyes than Swashki's had held, there was also a stronger lust, or perhaps something that should be called by a higher name.

"It is not I only," she said, "for whom you have cause to think. There may be some danger for me at the last, but it will be for Tela alike, and for each it may not be much. For our plan is that Tela, as she has told you, will lead those who go up by the inward way, as is right, for they are her caves, and the secret hers.

"I will go with those who ascend when the thorns are burnt, for it is I who thought of that place, and of that plan; while it is you who will lead the first attack on the coast cliffs, trusting to night and surprise, which has been your plan from the first.

"We shall each be in our own place, but while you will climb by a most perilous way, Tela will be without risk till they arrive on the higher land, which they are likely to find at first to be empty of any foe; and I suppose that there may be cover of smoke by which we can climb without being clearly seen, even though the apes may have reached the top by that time, which is less than sure."

Bwene looked ill content. "I see," he said, "why Tela must go, for she will lead a way which is known only to her."

"And there would be no doubt of the way that the thorns had burnt...? But it is a thing pledged to your own folk that I shall be seen there when the summit is won." She added: "It was not of my own wish. I have no will to die by an ape's teeth, which I have seen used.... But we do not think to stand at the front of war. We shall not strive with our own hands, either Tela or I. We shall be safe enough, unless you all fail."

She joined Tela's name, thinking that he should have care for both, as indeed he had, though his eyes were more busy with her. He had sense to see that the risk was no more than must ever be in the scales of war, in which the woman's stake is no less than that of the men, though it may differ in kind, and may be somewhat deferred. But, if the men die, the women must expect to do the same on the next day, unless they may be needed to breed, or as useful slaves, of which the chances are small when apes bicker with men who differ in shape and blood; or they may be kept awhile for a day of feast, if they will submit to fatten, and to feed well, which is no better end than to be slain in the heat of war.

There can be no safety in war except for those who end with their feet on their foemen's necks.

The King thought that there was no more to be said at that time, except such things as should be heard by those who waited without. Or, at least, nothing more on these matters of peril and war, but he remembered that he had resolved to ask Raina another thing, which he had asked the Old One in vain, and with little faith, for he had doubted much of all her priestly pretence since he had known how she had used his daughter to be her miraculous child.

"Goddess," he said, "you come from a gods' land, such as I have not thought nor beheld, even in the freedom of dreams, and you must know much that is hidden from lower eyes. I suppose that you can tell me this, if you will. Am I cursed that I have no son? And, if so, is it such a curse as may be lifted away?"

The question startled Raina, who had known no more than that he was a childless king (as was supposed). She did not guess that Tela was daughter to him, for all she had heard was from Tela's lips, who kept that to herself.

She felt it to be a question on which she had no wisdom to give, even had he told her much more than he did. Vaguely, she recalled disconnected, uncertain theories concerning the control of fertility of which she had heard or read, but she was not sure that men knew more than they had done when women had prayed the moon with a firm faith that it might give fruit to a barren womb.

Paradoxically, she thought, as she had done more than once in her talks with Tela, that as men learned more they knew less. It is easier to become sure that you are on a wrong road than to find one that is right....

Bwene lived in a world in which he was sure of many obvious things, most of which she knew to be illusions of mind or eye, or concerning which men had raised more doubts than they were able to solve. He was not puzzled as to the nature of matter, and he knew that the sun moved over the sky. She had been taught contrary things, which she had taken with equal trust, sure of her wisdom, and of the folly of earlier men, and another age might decide that they were an equal folly of childish minds....

But these things as they might, it was sure that she was no messenger from the clouds to confer pregnancy on an ageing wife. Bwene was in the full strength of mature years, but his wife might not be young. She asked: "Is your wife old?"

She had been silent for a moment, while her thoughts had come to this point, and his own mind had not been idle the while. He had a bold thought, which he would not have lacked courage to speak, but that he had the cares of a king, and had learned to restrain his moods, as one who would rule well must be practised to do. He dared not risk at this time that he should offend her who had so strangely appeared to give heart to a sickened land, but in two days' time, when the fight would be done.... He turned his mind to reply.

"She is not so old that she might not bear."

72

"Has she no children at all?"

"She had one, but—it died." He had paused in a reply which was not only a lie to his own mind, but which was known to be so by at least one of the two who heard. He had a fear lest Raina might be able to read his heart, which was not lessened by her reply, for she had seen a flicker of eyes, instant as it had been, and had noticed the second's pause in his words which would not have been but that he had suddenly come to a pit for which he had not been prepared, not having expected the question that she had put. She felt that there was a fact withheld, though she did not come near to a true guess as to what it might be, and it showed her a way to avoid a divination she could not give.

"Those," she said, "who seek wisdom of gods, must show their hearts in an open way, lest they be paid in the coin they use.... But I will tell you this. It has been seen at times that those whose children are few may increase at times, if they will change to another soil, though I will not say that I know why."

She did not think, after saying this, that she had shown any wisdom at all—not, at least, if she wished to be esteemed a goddess among these people, about which she was not sure. She should have framed her reply in a more oracular form, as Tela would have been careful to do.

But Bwene thought that she had read his mind more than she had. And, beyond that, he thought the oracle good. They were to conquer the ape-men's land, and then a child would be his. And he looked at Raina again, as he thought of whom he would choose its mother to be. What he said was: "Shall they come in?"

Tela, who had read both their minds as clearly as though they had been two of the tablets the Old One wrote, was not sure whether she should be vexed or pleased, but she saw, as Bwene had done, that such thoughts must be put aside for a better time.

"They can come in," she said. "I will fetch them now."

She rose and went out, leaving the King and Raina sitting side by side on the floor.

CHAPTER SIXTEEN

HAD one of Bwene's own people been asked as to the extent of his power, he would have replied that it was of an absolute kind, having the rights of life and death over all he ruled, and that there was none to resist his will. He would have believed that he spoke truth, and all who heard would have said the same. But Bwene himself, having pondered much, and so increased the natural wisdom which had been his portion at birth, knew that his power was constrained within narrow bounds, and that it kept its aspect of strength only because it did not test the limits that held it in.

He was bound by customs and traditions which were far stronger than he, to which his people bowed without challenge of thought. Even had he contemned them himself, which he was not always able to do, he knew well that the people would not have endured that they should be treated without respect.

Bira, being of strong will, and resolute that her own child should not drown, had transgressed one of the oldest customs that ruled the land, but she had done it by fraud and stealth; and though it had saved the life of one who was also his, she had not dared, in eighteen years, to tell him what she had done, nor had he asked in an open way. Yet it had become a knowledge which they shared without speech, and a shadow which would not lift, for he had come to think that the gods had cursed her to barren years for the trick by which she had crossed their will. It would have been hard for himself to say how much of the bitter spirit they had, which was near to hatred at times, had its roots in that defiance of unseen power, and how much in the disappearance of his two later wives, which he did not greatly doubt to lie at her door, though he had no proof, and had not therefore required the penalty due to so great a crime, being of a just and continent mind.

Yet they came together from time to time, for she had a fierce desire that he should have a son for his heir who should also be hers, and she had no fear of the gods herself, nor much belief in their power; and he would think that their wrath might tire, or that she might conceive at some time when they were careless of mood, or were looking another way.

When he asked himself why he felt toward her the hatred which was latent between their souls, even at times of an outward peace, he thought it was for those wives she had slain when they were pregnant by him; but he saw that he might even have forgiven their deaths had he had a son from herself, so that the deeper causes were hard to see.

But now he had a new scheme, and a new hope. He looked at Raina and thought: "If she be goddess in truth, the gods themselves might lack power or will to prevent, and if she be no more than a mortal from other lands, then it should be the surer that she will not oppose what I think to do. Yet it must wait for this day."

Raina, sitting but four feet away in the silent cave, and aware that his eyes and thoughts were centred upon herself, was glad to think that Tela's absence would not be long. She was conscious of that intimacy which comes to any two who are left alone together in a quiet place, but she did not think of the King as one she would ever wed. Nor, indeed, any man of this land, for they were not of her kind.

Yet, be her thoughts what they might, she had the under-consciousness that she was ever the object of Bwene's eyes, and that he had his own plans, which might be different from hers, but he made no motion toward her, and spoke no word, and there was soon the sound of Tela's return, leading in the two who had been waiting without.

The King told the two men to be seated before him, Tela and Raina sitting at his right hand, while he told the plans which had been made for the next night, adding details which need not be recorded here.

He said to Swashki: "It is you who will follow the way of the burning thorns. The goddess will go with you, so that you may be sure that events will fall in a fortunate way. But you will surround her with the best fighters you have, guarding her with a great care, for it is on her safety that all depends."

Swashki looked at Raina in his bold way, and said the King need have no fear about that.

He was a man of small brain, but a great conceit. So far, he had come through life with a swaggering mind, and none had guessed the depths of folly to which he might lightly fall. He had the courage of those whose bodies are healthy and strong and young. He was expert at all sports which require a firm hand, and a measuring eye. At the seal-fishing, he was called the first in the fleet. It was that which had brought him to where he was, among a people who were all unpractised in war.

The King gave him command because he was of repute in the fleet, and because he was one of those who had been prompt to come back from the fishing, which most who were there had been slow to do. It was Bwene's anxiety now that so many had not returned…

Swashki looked at Raina, and saw no more than his eyes could behold in a dim light. Priestess or goddess were words of little meaning for him. His universe was himself, and the pleasant things he wanted and took. Now he had a treasonous thought, the audacity of which went beyond any distant, half-formed design in the King's mind.

He saw that the main assault was to be at the seaward cliffs, where the King would lead, and he had no doubt that a king can die. He thought he would be very likely to die, before the apes would give ground to those who ventured that hard ascent.

And it would be his own part to lead men who would have a screen of smoke to cover them when they climbed, and at a time when it was likely that the full force of the apes would be engaged in combat with those whom the King would be leading twelve miles away…. He saw himself as the leader of men who made spectacular triumph at less cost than would be the portion of most. Or perhaps leading his separate force to some distant land, after the King had been repulsed in the main attack…. The apes would be between him and retreat. It might be safer to go on than to fight his way back. The apes might be content to see him go off by a further way, which he would be very willing to do, for who would wish to fight hard to return to so sick a land…? Or the apes might be scattered and slain, and the King dead; and a new king must be found, for he had no son. In such times, where should men look for a king, among those who are already chosen as leaders of war?

Swashki had gone through the first years of life picking up all he would in an easy way, as though for him it were no less than a natural law, as (had he been equal to so much thought) he might have judged it to be. He did not doubt that life would continue by equally pleasant and easy paths. He looked at Raina again, and thought that his three wives (who had been enough to content him until today) could be missed without much regret. Certainly, he would guard her well.

Raina looked at Plini and him, and her choice would have been the man with the single eye, but she had no fear of Swashki, whom she did not value at his own price. She may have had less fear than she should.

Plini had listened to this point without speech, which it was not his habit to waste. Now he said: "When a plan is fixed, it is well to speak none but very confident words, lest we weaken the hearts of men. Is it thus I should speak here, or do we take counsel with open minds?"

"You should speak your thoughts," the King answered, knowing him to be cool in judgment, and not one to be shaken by easy fear.

"Then I will say that those whom I lead will take long to deploy, if they should come out, as I suppose, through a narrow hole; and they will be without means of retreat except at the same pace. It may go ill if the flame of the burning thorn shall call a great force of apes, which may come upon us while we are not fully out and arrayed; for, as I understand, we may come out in the very midst of the way between the coastal attack and that which Swashki will lead."

Swashki said: "I call that a dull thought. Why, you will be expecting them, not they you! Why should you not suppose that they will pass some distance away, and, while they hurry to our attack, you will be a sudden terror around their rear?"

Plini showed no resentment at Swashki's tone, though it had not been far from contempt. He said: "I meant no more than that those I lead should start at an early hour, that they may be arrayed for strife while the dawn is young."

"That," said the King, "is how it shall be. Have you more to say?"

"You will think me of poor heart," Plini replied, looking at Swashki, but not as one who cared much what he might think, either of evil or good, "but I would attack this night, even now, if we could make head before dawn, as I think we might. For the wind moves to the south."

Swashki stared, not seeing at once what could be the meaning of that, but the King answered: "It is a thought I already had, but it must be chanced, for we cannot attack this night. There are too many who are not back…. Is there yet more?"

Plini said no to that. He had another thought in his mind, but he judged that it was in the King's also, and that it had been answered before he spoke. He reflected that such doubts must be in the minds of all leaders of men when they are on the threshold of war, and that it may be that those who are most anxious at first may come out best in the end. From which thought he took what comfort he could.

He knew that the preparations which had been made already had caused some stir in the land, the meaning of which might not be guessed by those they planned to attack, but there had been disquieting signs that the apes had been watching from the cliff tops during the day. He would have attacked that night, had he had his will, without regard for those who were not there, but he saw that the King was not blind, and might need no counsel from him.

Bwene had pondered the same thought, but he knew it would not be easy to get the people to move before the hour that the oracle had announced, and he was hoping that another day would increase his strength, for there were still nearly a thousand men who were away at the fishing, and who might still return by the next day, as they had been summoned to do.

Seeing that Plini had done, he turned to Tela to say: "If it be now agreed, I will go, having many cares for this night. We must believe that it will come to a good end, the gods having declared their will."

When they had gone, Raina, who supposed that they might be less certain than the King thought to come to a good end, if they had no better support than a declaration of supernatural will, asked, with some anxiety in her tone: "What is this about the south wind?"

"It brings rain," Tela replied. "What they meant was—if it is wet, will the thorns burn?"

"I cannot say that. They are brittle now."

She saw that, if Swashki's force should be unable to make the ascent, she would have no praise. She would be less goddess than public fool, when she might have seemed wise with nothing harder than silence to learn.

"Oh, well," Tela said, "it may not rain for a week."

CHAPTER SEVENTEEN

THE next day there were heavy clouds in the sky, and the wind rose. The two girls were alone in the cave, to which no one came, for all were busy in preparations which must be carried on with as little indication of what they were as could be contrived, for it had become plain that they were watched from the higher land, which it was no pleasure to know.

The two who were in the cave were not vexed for that, they having had no word of what was passing without, but Raina saw the menace of rain, and was often at the mouth of the cave, looking up at a glooming sky. She saw that it might rain as it would, and the attack succeed none the less, but it would make folly of her plan, and of herself, as having given it birth, which none had asked her to do.

About noon, a shower fell, but was soon done. After dark, rain fell for an hour. It had ceased when Huni came to the cave mouth, though the sky was still closed with cloud.

"The King asks," he said, "is all well? For there will be no moon to guide those who climb if these clouds prevail."

Tela understood that she was required to send some inspiriting word. She answered: "Did I say that the moon would show? If those who climb can see no more than their own feet, will they not be safe from above?"

Huni went back to interpret her words as she had meant that he should. "The priestess says that the gods have chosen a night of cloud, so that there shall be less peril for those who climb."

The hours of the night went by, and the time came when Swashki's men, moving quietly, and two abreast, began to ascend the gorge.

After them, Swashki himself, and then Plini came to the cave. At this time, it was raining again. Plini said: "The thorns will surely be wet. Were it not better that we should all go by the one way?"

But Swashki had no will to give up his separate command, to follow at Plini's tail. Also, he remembered what Plini had urged about the slowness with which his men would emerge, and the impossibility, of rapid retreat, however needful it might become. He might have taken it in a light way at the time, but if he himself were to be involved, it became a matter for more serious thought. He had a vision of men who had become a mob fighting to pass through a narrow hole, which themselves blocked, while the apes slaughtered around their rear.

He said that it was not for them to alter a plan which a goddess made.

Raina, hearing, was not sure that he did not sneer, and the doubt resolved her not to swerve from her own plan, unless with more certainty of mistake than she then had.

After that, the men who were to ascend the caves began to arrive. Tela had gone ahead, and Plini next behind her. Raina stood beside Swashki, watching the men file through. His own force had now passed up the gorge, and were drawn under some shelter of hanging cliff somewhat above the place of thorns where they were to attempt ascent. Swashki said that there was no reason to go himself till the dawn should be very near. He talked to Raina at times, but got little reply. She did not always understand what he said, and at times would have been content to understand less. She had no mind to become familiar to him.

She wore a woman's cloak, for which Tela had sent at her request, there being no such garment within the cave. To obtain this, she had made pretext of the rain, and that it might be cold in the night hours.

She saw that she would make a poor goddess, if she should appear to people who had not seen her before, in a wet cloak, like a draggled bird, but she supposed that they would only see her if the victory had become theirs, and what would anything matter then? They would be content though they did not see her at all.

Besides, she had made no claim to the divinity which had been thrust upon her. The idea had an aspect of unreality, of unimportance, beside that of the conflict for which they were waiting now.... The rain had ceased again, and the moon showed, a dim white disc behind covering cloud. Swashki said it was time to go, and she went with him up the river path by which she had first come to the cave....

It might have been better to have begun to fire the thorn at an earlier hour. It did not refuse to light, but it burnt in a slow, smouldering way, with a dense smoke which did not rise, but drifted backward and down the canyon, so that it was soon choked with a denser gloom than had been that of the clouded night. Still, it burned; and, as it became cool enough to be followed up, it was found that, even if the bushes were not wholly consumed, the points of their thorns had gone, so that they were no longer a menace to those who climbed.

With the time that the burning took, and the great height that there was to scale, it was more than two hours after dawn when the top was reached, and then it was found that the level of the plateau was still above, for they were in one of those clefts of the plain, such as Raina had known at the first, where the ape-men dwelt.

There was no sign as yet that their coming had been observed, nor was there much wonder in that, for the smoke could not have risen at any time to the height of the plain above, a wind coming out of the upper gorge, as it rose to that height, and beating it backward and down.

The sides of this upper gorge were too steep to be easily scaled, and as the men climbed over the brink they were ranged in column, and marched along it, seeking the better way of escape that there was likely to be at its upper end. It was plain that it was a place where the ape-men came, for it was filled with those trees the fruit of which was their main food, which should have been loaded with ripened crops at this season, but they were bare, having been lately stripped

About a mile up the gorge, they came to a group of the ape-men's huts, which they thought to be deserted at first, but they found, on a search being made, two of their young, less than half-grown, hidden away, which they killed, and then found others lurking among the trees, which they chased, and slew; but they were left in doubt of whether some might not have escaped to carry warning above, which caused them to push on at a better pace than before.

They found also a storehouse of fruit, which Swashki detailed twenty men to remove, getting it down the cliff by the best method they could contrive; thinking that, at the worst, he would thus have something to show for his part.

Raina met these men bearing their burdens back, for, at Swashki's urgent desire, she had been one of the last to ascend, and was now surrounded by a guard who closed her in on all sides. It was the first time she had seen the men of this race, except such as had come to the cave. They were clothed in loose garments, coarse and white, and with scarlet trimmings which might have more mean-

THE VENGEANCE OF GWA, BY S. FOWLER WRIGHT

ing than she could read, but they had little semblance of martial array, nor defensive cover of any kind, such as would delay an ape's spear, or its rending teeth, except that many were muffled around the neck.

Most of them carried fish-bone spears, and some had wooden clubs, in which flintheads had been sunk, making then weapons not to be lightly faced.

The men did not show a very bold mien. She thought them nervous, and that each had less confidence in himself than in his comrades on either hand, but she could not tell how natural that might be among such as go into a strange war. She was aware that her own heart beat at times at a faster pace than it should, which she was anxious should not be guessed.

CHAPTER EIGHTEEN

THE clouds cleared, as the sun came. They advanced over a level plain, the surface of which was yellow, and dried, and bare, and had no shelter at all. If there had been rain here in the night, it had been sucked in with such thirst that its signs were gone, though it was but three hours after the dawn. The high level plateau, with its dome of unbroken sky, was more strange to Swashki and those he led even than to Raina who had once seen it before.

They would have made better progress now, had they not been hindered by the frequent fissures that broke the level surface of the plain; but they discovered that these giant clefts did not invariably continue to the limit of the plateau, being sometimes of quite moderate extent, the ground opening and closing again in a gap which might be no more than a mile in length or much less. But they were alike in that they all took the same parallel course, and were of the same depth, varying only in length, and to a less extent in the width to which they had split open, as it seemed that they must have done in some paroxysm of once-molten or frozen rock.

Circumventing one of these, and laboriously descending another, and ascending it on the further side, they came on the first evidence of the strife which had already disturbed the quietude of that sun-baked plain. They saw the scattered corpses of apes and men that lay ahead and somewhat leftward over a trampled ground. The apes lay as they had fallen, showing the causes of their deaths in a broken skull or the thrust of a fish-bone spear. But the blood-sucked bodies of the more human dead, flaccid and torn, showed not only the ways of their bestial foes, but, too clearly, who must have been left in possession of that disputed ground.

Swashki halted his march, as he looked down on the broken dead. Following their trail with his eyes, he saw some movement upon the plain, it might be a mile away. He made a good guess at what it would be likely to mean. Plini's force had emerged at an earlier hour, had been driven back, and were now attempting to regain safety by retreating the way they came. Apes moved on the edge of a canyon which might now be a cauldron of bitter strife, or of the mere slaughter of those who jostled to enter a narrow hole.

When he considered this, and that there had been no advance from the seaward assault, where the King should have made ascent some four hours before, it was easy to decide that the apes had had the better of a strife which he might be too late to change. There was a temptation to march back while he yet could.

But he was not a physical coward, and he cared much for his own esteem in the mouths of men. He looked round at comrades who seemed to be of somewhat better heart than before. That which the ground bore had roused them to a fury of hatred against the apes, which made courage an easier thing, anger being ever a foe to fear.

He spread his men in a five-deep line, which was as much of order as they were likely to keep. He admonished them to come on at a good pace, but not such as would break their array. He shouted to Raina's guard to keep somewhat behind, which they may have thought a good place. He led on with a flourished spear.

As he went forward thus, a new imagination came to his mind. He would destroy the apes whom he supposed to be baiting Plini now, but who would not be able to face on two fronts, and he being above them on the pit edge. Plini's men, even those who might have regained the caves, would come back, hearing of the rescue that he had made. He would have all the honour of that. Then, with the double force, he would march on to take those apes in the rear who might still be striving against the King. Here again, it would be by him that the scale of victory would incline to his own side. He would share the honour with none, for what could Plini say, but that he had saved him from shame and death? And, besides, Plini might be dead now. His eyes searched the ground as he went on for that which he might not desire, but which would have brought him no grief.... The King might be dead too.

It was his nature to think rather of the deaths of others than that his own throat might be torn by an ape's teeth. With a better wit, he might have gone far....

They were seen before they came to the edge of the pit, and the high warning cry of the apes, in that language which Raina had heard before, and resolved she could never learn, rose over the turmoil that raged below.

Swashki found that he was not to look down on foes who must scramble up to meet the thrust of the fish-bone spears. They came swarming out, showing that whatever the pit might hold did not require all their care. They came on at a run, and with no front of array, male and female alike, and some not much more than half grown. Few of them bore any arms, which might discommode those who would use all fours for comfort, or for change of effort, if they should run far. There were some who had wooden spears, but they seemed rather to be of a ceremonial significance than an increase of fighting strength. There were not more than eight score that came out from the pit's edge, but they advanced as having no fear at all.

Swashki halted his line, ordering that it should show a close front, as it was willing to do. The apes halted when they were five paces away, till they had all come up, squatting in a straight line. Their small eyes glowed red in ferocious hate, and the lust to kill; and their upper lips were withdrawn in a snarling way, showing teeth that were strong and white.... An ape screamed command, and the line sprang.

The apes did not rush on their human foes, as they may have been expected to do. They launched themselves through the air, taking such harm as they must from the thrust of a fishbone spear, if it should be directed by steady hands. But even if they met the point, as few did, the impetus of the leap would bear down the man from whom they might have taken a wound, and he would struggle beneath a vicious snarling weight that would tear him with teeth and hands, even though it might be losing some of its own blood.

Swashki, having moved somewhat behind to marshal his line, saw that his front rank was thrown to the ground by that leap, some of them bearing backward also the men behind, where they had been standing close in support. The whole front of his force had become a flurry that rolled and struggled upon the ground, some of the men behind thrusting in with their spears boldly enough, as a cook stirs in a pot. Then there came again that high shrill cry of command, and the apes drew back, except only such as could not get themselves free, and so they crouched again for another spring.

It seemed to Swashki that the half of his front line, if not more, lay still on the yellow stubble that was the grass of that land, or were twisting there in the prelude of death, and there were not more than eight or ten of the apes that had been too sore hurt to draw back when the signal called. He saw that it would not take many of such leaps to turn his command into no more than a flying rabble for the apes to slay as fast as they could pursue.

It was a case where attack was the best defence, and he raised a battle shout such as might have burst the lungs of a weaker man, as he rushed at the ape which was nearest to where he stood. The creature dodged the first thrust of the spear, seeking to pass it to reach his throat, which would have been his own end; but he had not won his name in the spearing of seals without cause, and he was adroit enough to retract his point in a lightning way, getting it in under the throat at the second thrust, which the leaping ape failed to avoid; and after that he held off a fury of snarling hate by the spear's length, till the point came out at the back of the ape's neck, and its strength went.

The most of the line were less quick than he, and few were able to use their spears with an equal skill, but they followed the lead he gave, so that the apes must close without the impetus of their deadly leaps. Had they been one to one, it could have made no difference in the end, for it was clear that an ape, using hands and jaw, could not be matched by a spear-armed man; but the men were three or four to the apes' one at all points, and if the man in front found that his spear broke in an ape's grip, or that he was borne to the ground, there would be relief from other spears that would thrust past him to right and left.

So, after there had been some moments of a fierce hustle of swaying strife, it was the apes that gave ground, and then there was another cry of command, and those that still had legs in sufficient use were running off as fast as they could bear them away, with Swashki's men hard and eager upon their tracks.

Meanwhile, Plini, who had been much in the posture that Swashki guessed, but who had found that the apes could be better checked in a place of trees than on open ground, and having felt the relief that came when a third of his foes had been drawn off to Swashki's attack, had made some head against those who remained. He had retreated in good order enough, when he had seen it to be the best thing he could hope to do, bearing off his wounded, whom he would not leave for the apes to tear; and he had passed these in safety back into the caves, and was retiring the rest of his force in a steady way when he changed his mind on seeing that by which he judged Swashki was approaching to his relief. He had attacked those apes that remained with a vigour which left them little heart for a fresh front, when their comrades came tumbling down the side, with Swashki's men not more than ten paces behind.

Now it was the apes that scuttered and dodged, having foes above and below, who were the more relentless and keen to slay for the fears through which they had passed themselves in the last hour. Soon there was nothing left to be done but to watch the flight of those whose legs would save them for that time, and to count the cost of such victory as they had united to win.

Swashki could say that he had come to the rescue of Plini's force, though he might have been glad to think that it had been less able to guard itself than the issue showed; but Plini lived, and being still in command of his own men, he must be asked what it was now his purpose to do.

"As to that," he said, "I would not fail to succour the King, even though it were at a great cost, or with little hope that we should come free, but I doubt that he can have endured on his part till this hour. You should know that these apes who attacked us here were no more than a separate band, which, as it appeared, were behind those who had been assembled to the defence of the cliff, and who came upon us to a common surprise, as we were but a short time forth. But there must have been knowledge of our design, as to the main attack, for the whole land, as you will have seen, is empty of apes, they having assembled, as I suppose, to meet the attack at the sole place where they would expect it to be."

"Then," Swashki asked, "you would go back without knowledge of how the King fares?"

"Yes, I would. You may call me coward, if you will. I might give you a different word if we had any easy retreat, but, if we should go on to meet with, I will not say the whole nation of apes, but a larger force than we have slain here, I do not see how the men would escape by the ways we have."

Swashki saw that there was reason in that. They had met but a few apes, and they had lost not less than three hundred men, beside those who were not so hurt but they could still stand. If they should be assailed by a great force, and far from their own retreats, they would surely be sped; and now that they knew how the apes could fight, and that they were assembled before the King commenced his attack, it seemed but a slender hope that he could have succeeded in his assault; and when they thought of the time which had gone since it must have commenced, and that there was no sign of his coming, a slender hope became none.

Swashki resolved that they should retire, but he was content that it should be by Plini's word, rather than his. He said: "Yet, if the King had been quickly sped, would the apes be still there? Would there be none to return from an ended strife?"

Plini did not answer that. He had a thought which was best unsaid. Also, he understood Swashki, to whom he gave a straight glance with his one eye, as he asked: "Well, shall it be forward or back?"

"It must be back, if you so advise."

"That I do." As he said this, Plini's one eye fell somewhat sourly on Tela and Raina, where they stood talking apart. "Unless," he added, "you will take counsel of higher powers."

Swashki did not reply. He may have understood that the suggestion was not gravely meant. In their different ways, they were both irreligious men, and they would have agreed that war was not women's work. Plini might have added that it was listening to them that had brought that war, which would have been less than just.

It was clear that, if retreat were to be made, there would be no gain in delay. It was agreed that the whole force should retire by the way of the caves, if there should be time for them to enter in single file before the apes should appear. Tela went first, as she had come, being their guide, and Raina went next to her. The way was long, and in a black darkness, so that even Tela could not have seen much. There was a wall on one side at most times, which Tela could feel, having one hand free, but at others there would be none, and then she would count her steps. There were places where it was very steep.

When they got back to the Sacred Cave, they were conscious of much fatigue, and glad to sit on the sealskin floor, watching the men file through, as it seemed, in a string which would never end. There was some crowding and confusion as the numbers grew, there being but narrow space without, between river and cliff, and the men bickering as to what their leaders had told them to do, until, at the last, Plini and Swashki came, and they were brought to order, and marched away.

Plini came back to speak to Tela before he left. "I am not at ease," he said, "concerning the entrance above. Holding hands, as you had required us to do, there could be none left to hide, or even close it against our foes, who will be likely to follow when they see where we must have come up."

Tela was unmoved about that. She said: "Let them try. They will come to no good."

"Well," he replied, "you should know.... I have put a strong guard up the stream, at a narrow place, lest the apes should come down where the thorns are burned, and should do you wrong.... I have told them, if they should be attacked, to send a runner at once to you, in which case you should leave here, and go, as I suppose, to the King's caves, which are more strong than the houses of men."

Tela asked: "Do you think they will come down?"

"I do not know what they will do. I am not one to whom the gods talk."

Tela did not know how to take that, but she saw that his deeds were those of a friend.

He went out, and the two were left alone in the cave, where they remained most of the day, being glad to rest, and being roused by none until the sun was low in the sky, when Huni came from the King.

CHAPTER NINETEEN

TELA saw Huni approach, for she had gone to look forth as the day waned. It was time for the offerings of men to be brought to the cave mouth, but they had not come.

She said, before Huni could speak: "You shall come into the cave, and sit there at ease, for you will have much to tell, and the news, as I suppose, is not good."

Huni did not deny that: He had the look of a weary man, who would be glad to sit on a soft floor.

When he was set, Tela said: "You need not tell that the King failed. Was the loss great?"

"Priestess," Huni replied, "it would seem that you know much by your own ways."

Raina, who knew that Tela had made no more than an easy guess, saw that she did not mean to let her prestige fail without an effort for its defence.

"There is no hurt," Tela rejoined, "if I hear twice. Tell me what I have asked."

"Priestess, there were men of courage who reached the top. It would have been well had there been less, for they are dead now. But the most did not go so far, there being a rain of rocks, beneath which they were crushed or bruised, if they did not die. It was a rain that did not slacken, and was not easy to face."

"How did the King fare?"

"He has an arm torn by an ape's teeth, so that no man can say that he was not bold, and active to reach the top."

"Were the apes many or few?"

"Priestess, he would have you know that they were a swarm covering all the land. He had not thought them to be so many, not by a one to their ten, but he will not say this aloud, lest men murmur more than they now do. It was a sight which few saw, and most of those are now dead."

"And you will tell me that those who live have lost heart for this war?"

"Priestess, so it is; nor do they call it an evil themselves can stay. There is fear that we have started a war that we cannot stop. The apes remain on the cliff. They look down, as those who talk of taking a prey. And the people murmur against the King, and against you. They say that the Old One would have given them a more fortunate word."

"Then if they do not want my words, why do you come here?"

"The King seeks a new word, such as may turn them again."

Tela considered this. "Huni," she asked, "should men approach the gods at a light need?"

"None can say we did that, for our need was sore."

"At a great need, should we not use our own strength, or should we sleep, that the gods may aid us the more?"

"Priestess, I should say that we fought as well as men may be expected to do."

"And what of those who were not there?"

Huni saw her meaning when she asked that. There were those who had loitered at the fishing, being in no haste to leave it, nor, it may be, to join the war to which they were called.

"There are many," he said, "who are still away; and there are some who have returned since the sun rose; and they murmur the most of all that they have come back to a periled land."

"They are men," Tela replied, "whose mouths should be very still, for the wrath of the gods is active about their feet.... But you will say this to the King. We did not fail, neither the goddess nor I. We went where we had said, walking at will on the upper land, and there was slaughter of those who opposed our paths. But the gods will lift no weights for those who use but one arm. My word is that there is still hope, but it is not equal for all. They who are loyal to those who lead, and are valiant of mood, will yet come to a fertile land; but those who doubt may find that they have as much cause as their fears protest."

Huni pondered on this. He had his own doubts, among which were some that should not be spoken aloud, being of her to whom he had come now. But he saw that Tela had answered shrewdly enough.

"Priestess," he said, "it is a good word, though it whip the weak."

"It is the best they will get.... Is the King sore hurt?"

"His wound has been cleansed and dressed, and his wits are his. But his arm is swollen and hot."

"You will tell him that we must talk, for the land's gain. But as he is hurt, we will come to him. I will come when the moon shows over the gorge; by which hour I would have a good guard waiting here from the King."

Huni said it was well, and returned without more delay.

"You spoke a word," Raina said, when they were alone again, "such as should shut the mouths of those who murmur, either against you or the King."

Tela showed no pleasure at being praised. "I sent," she said, "no more than a poor lie. I do not think we could have broken the apes had they returned to the last man, or a thousand more. But it was the best I could say…. We must see the King, for I do not know what his present purpose may be, and we must speak with one mouth."

After that, she was active to order the cave, which would be left to itself for the first time since her own birth, and for how long before that she could make no guess. There were things which she would not risk to come to the eyes of men, and which must be hidden away, being carried into dark inward recesses where it was a small chance that any would find both them and their own way back.

She looked at the secret tablets, and considered that none could read them except herself, but they might be injured or lost. With Raina's help, she sunk those that she valued most in a shallow pool, from which she thought that it would be easy to get them again, as she was not destined to do; so that they may lie there to this day.

When these things had been done, and they had eaten from such stale food as they still had, they went out, to find that the King had sent the guard for which Tela had asked.

Raina said: "You would have me come?"

"Would you stay here?" Tela replied. "I suppose we may not be long before we return."

Raina said that they would go the same way of her will, for she felt that she had one friend in the land, but not more.

CHAPTER TWENTY

THEY found that the men who waited outside the cave were under Swashki's command. He was careful to say that he had not come only to bring the escort for which Tela had asked, as though his importance had become too great for that in the last day. He had brought relief to those whom Plini had set to watch the gorge, and these were the men that he was now leading away. Tela listened to this, making little reply, and Raina, who felt herself to be no more than a pawn in a game that she did not play, said nothing at all.

They went by a way that Tela was supposed not to have traversed before, but which she knew by night, it may be, somewhat better than those by whom she was now led. They feared the dark as much as an active foe, but they knew it to be a fear that the apes did not share, and it was the measure of the new dread that had fallen upon the land that men were still moving abroad for defence in the midnight hours.

They came to the Cave of Words, where it had been the King's use to sit often during the day, and where he would deal justice, and take counsel at times, but which it was the law that none should enter, except he called him by name. It was another sign of the terror which had fallen upon the land, and of a slackened fear of the King's name, that Swashki should lead them in as he did, as though he entered the house of a common man.

He had become of some sudden repute during the day, as one who had been in the upper land, and had defeated the apes, which had appeared to be of an invincible strength to those who had approached them on hands and knees, struggling up the side of the seaward cliffs. There were different tales of what his exploits had been; for some of those he had led, and who had come back alive, were inclined to boast of what they had done, as men who had chastened foes.

They exalted themselves, and the name of their leader rose in the same breath. But others would speak more of the great strength of the apes, and of how few there had been that they had encountered and overcome, and at how great a cost of their own lives. Yet it was agreed in all mouths that Swashki had played the part of a man, and that his leadership had not failed. Besides that, there was the store of fruit he had seized, which the King had ordered to be distributed to the people at large. He is victor who takes the spoils, and this fruit was the one gain they had for the blood that the day had cost, and the fear of what might be to come. Swashki's name stood high at this hour, and he was not stirred to surprise that men should esteem him at such a worth.

He walked into the Cave of Words, where the King sat with a bandaged arm, but upright enough, and disregarding the fatigue which must have been his at this hour. Swashki, who had found time for his own sleep in the later day, looked round on men who had travailed more, and were less content with what they had been able to do.

For the King was not sitting alone; he was the centre of a group who thought themselves of enough worth to be there, whether called or not, of whom some were as plain and bitter of speech as men may dare in the face of a king in whose hands the power of death may still be, but who has brought ruin upon the land. And over all was the shadow of urgent fear.

Tela looked round, and would have found it easy to wish that she had not come. She had a different fear from that which disturbed the hearts of those whose bickerings fell to a sudden silence of curiosity and surprise, as she and Raina entered the lighted cave. She was timid by nature, and young in years, and most unused to stand in an assembly of men. She had thought to come to the King alone, to gain knowledge, and to agree such plans as would strengthen them both for the next day. She would have found it easy to feel afraid, but she controlled herself from any signal of that.

The King sat in his great chair, which had been hammered out of a protrusion of rock at the upper end of the cave. There were no other chairs, but the floor of the cave, which was unlevel in a curious wave-like form, had been smoothed and hollowed into shapes in which men could sit, if they were so allowed by the King, when they would be much lower than he.

The floor was soft with the sealskins which were the carpet luxury of that land. The roof was a ragged dome, which the lights did not clearly reveal. From the place where the King sat, the words of a man who spoke in a high tone would ascend, and wander about as though seeking escape which they could not find.

This was a wonder the King would not often use, except when he might at times be alone, and would test how its sound could be best obtained. It seemed that there was a god there who was friendly to him, and who would confirm his words at the appeal of a lifted voice.

The King rose up when he saw who had entered the cave, which was the greatest honour that he could pay: and he cried, "Hail!" in a high voice, so that the greeting came again from the hollow roof, causing men to look up in a sudden dread.

There may be a doubt that he would have risen thus had the Old One entered the cave, or that he would have appealed to the god in the high roof, to add his voice to his own, for he had been jealous of his power as against hers; but he felt differently to Tela, and also that they were now allied as against dangers, both from abroad, and from those whose loyalty had become unsure. It was an aid to his own strength that men should give honour to her.

The King's wife sat on a long ledge which was to the right of his throne, she being the only woman within the cave. He called to Tela and Raina that they should come to sit at the same place, which Tela was very willing to do.

Bira was clothed in a garment of seaweed green, which may have been the most precious thing that the land held, it being stained with a dye which was very hard to obtain, and that with much labour, and then only drop by drop. It was a sign of rank without power.

The King had on a loose cloak, brightly red, being alike in colour to the close-fitting dress that Tela wore at such times as she would be seen by men, as she did now. It was the sign of power, which none could wear except she and the King. All the men who had come to the cave wore white garments banded with red, and closed with a red stone at the throat. These stones were of little account, for they could be picked up freely upon the shore, and men will put value only on that which is hard to get, but they could not be so worn, except by men of a certain rank, so that it was plain that those who intruded there were not of the common kind, though they might be much less than the King.

Bira looked at Raina in an instant way, which saw much; but she had no time to linger on her, seeing her own child for the first time since it had left her arms in a space of few days from its birth. Her eyes softened somewhat from the hard courage with which they were used to look on a hated world, being gladdened by what she saw. The eyes of mother and daughter met, so that there was a time in which they forgot the moment in which they lived, being aware of each other, and nothing else. And then Bira rose, and moved somewhat away from the King, so that Tela would take a seat which would be of more honour than hers. It was no more than the Old One would have claimed, as her right of rank, had she condescended to come to the King at all, but it is less sure that the Queen would have agreed with a good will.

Now she looked again, and made a further movement, though it may have been with less will, so that there would be space for two at the King's side, and Tela sat down next to her, leaving to Raina the place of most honour, nearest the King.

The King observed this in a tired mind, in which courage only remained, rather than power to think or to plan. He had been awake for two days of anxious and busy cares: he had led the assault up the steep cliffs, and was one of few who had gained the brink, and almost the only one who had returned from it alive, and with the knowledge that an ape had died when his club struck: he had a long gash on the upper arm, with pain and fever therefrom: he beheld men enter the Cave of Words with less respect for himself than he had supposed he would ever see, but he did not order them forth, nor say that he needed rest, for he had thought that treason would be less bold under his own eye than if it plotted apart, and he thought still to maintain himself, and to bring all to a good end; it was not his fault that he could not think with a clear mind.

He was glad to see Tela enter the cave, and to observe the silence that fell thereat among men the most of whom had not seen her before, nor yet the stranger sight of the white goddess who moved as one being at ease, and yet remote from themselves. He had a thought of what he would say now, and was not aware how the moments passed as he sat still, for he had lost contact of time; and in the silence a man, Ooli by name, who had come from the fishing only a few hours before, and who had been loudest in complaint against those who had started this useless, perilous war, approached to where Tela sat, and addressed her in a tone in which new insolence strove with an old respect, and both with an urgent fear:

"Priestess, as you are here, you have come to guide us as we suppose, and there is but one thing we would know. Will the apes descend upon us this night, or have we got till the dawn to cast hawsers, and sail away?"

Tela did not know how different was the demeanour of those who were in the cave from that which was usual around the King, it all being strange to her; but she knew that the man spoke without the humility which the Old One had expected to be observed to herself, whose mantle she now wore: she had been warned by Huni that authority shook, in which she saw that the King and she must warm their hands at the same fire: she saw the look in her mother's eyes as Ooli approached, from which she judged that he would not live long if Bira could have her will: and she saw that her father the King was a sick man, which he strove that he should not show. She was aware of a great fear, and she had not learned herself long enough to know that she was bravest when most afraid. She rose up to reply:

"I know our lord the King, and Huni, through whom he speaks, and some others, who are good men; but you are one whom I do not know.... You would go down on your face and lie long, before I would give you any answer at all.... But I will tell you that which you have not asked, that if you talk of sailing away, not having the King's order therefore, it will matter little to you that the apes may come, for you will have felt your end before then in the place where those who have found the wrath of the King are led out to die."

She turned her eyes from a man whose truculence was not enough to outface the new fear that her words proposed, and addressed those who were silent around:

"But I will ask you this. When the apes found that they were too strong to be driven back from the cliff verge, why did they not descend in their wrath to make a prey of our land, we having provoked the war? And if you cannot reply, I may do that too.

"There would be those who came to them in a flying haste, showing wounds, and crying that foes were abroad, though they could not say from where they had come. They would send to see, and there would come back a tale of dead, it may be a score of scores, scattered over the land. Would they not be more slow to descend, not knowing what may be raging behind their rear...? I led some of you by a secret way, and we have walked in the apes' land, and have come back, having slain our foes. It is true that we have found a harder foe than some thought, and that there are urgent causes for counsel of those who are round the King. But it is not your foes whom you have most greatly to fear, it is they who are faint of heart, or make wisdom weak—it is those who may wreck the land."

As she ceased, the King rose. Her words had reached his mind, so that he had become more aware of himself, and of a weakness he must not show.

"You have heard good words," he said, "such as the gods send to those for whom they would still care. You may see thereby that they have not cursed our race, but those only of feeble hands and disloyal hearts, of whom I will not think there are more than a few. But this talk is done. At a short space after dawn, I hold counsel here with such as I call by name at that time."

He held himself erect with a strong will as he stepped down from his seat, and men who had, for a moment, been silenced by Tela's words, gave way before him, so that it seemed that he drove them forth, like a shepherd rounding his flock, being helped thereto by those who were still of a loyal heart, and were active to do his will.

He looked at Tela, and at the Queen, and it was easy to see that they were of good accord. He said to Tela: "You will wait here for this time? There is much to plan, but my mind strays."

He went out, with Huni next at his side, to his private cave. Huni was troubled that he should be alone there in the night, but he would have his way about that.

"Do you think me slain?" he asked. "Well, I am not. I lack sleep and blood. You will place a guard of men you can trust. They must face the dark. Call me aloud, if the apes enter the land, but for nothing less; and if you call, I will come. And have food ready for when I wake, for I suppose that I shall eat much."

He entered the cave, and closed it with the stone that could not be moved, except on the inner side. He was alone there, whether for life or death, and he sank into instant sleep....

The Queen said to Tela: "You will stay with me this night," to which she quickly agreed, though it was not what she had intended to do. The invitation was for Raina alike, she being jointly with Tela there. Beyond that, the Queen did not regard her at all.

Bira's cave, which was the same she had had when Tela was born, was lofty, and furnished well, and was kept alight through the darker hours. She gave Tela a couch which was next her own, and they talked long. They did not hide the nearness of blood which they both knew, though there was much which a common prudence would keep from being uttered aloud.

Tela slept at length, and the Queen's mind wandered back to distant, unforgettable things. She remembered how she had schemed and sinned that another babe might die, and her own live to be sleeping beside her now. Even the King could not blame her greatly for that, when he looked at his living child, who had such beauty of form, and a wisdom beyond her youth.

Her mind wandered to darker ways, when she thought of those other wives whom she had lured during the night to the secret place, the deep cavern where their bones must now lie, in that black lake where sunlight could never come.

She had thought then that she did well, or rather she had not cared were it well or ill, should it only succeed, and be free from proof as against herself. She had thought then that she would bear a male child before long, and it would live to be King, though a dozen mothers should die before they had time to bear.... But as the years passed, and she was not pregnant again, she had some belief that she might have been cursed to barrenness by indignant gods, as she knew that Bwene thought her to be—and when the land sickened—and now that this war had proved more than they were likely to win.... Was it the chastising of gods? Was it the vengeance of Gwa...? Well, there would still be a good thought. Even gods do not bring back the dead. Could she not tire them at last with her own resolve? Could they not be reasonable, and accept a fact that they could not change, letting her have a babe even now...? Her thoughts took a sombre tone, she not having much hope about that.... Yet she did not admit defeat, nor did she plead, for she was not of those who look up, or who will cajole, or pray for their own gain. She argued and strove, with a stubborn unyielding will, which was still bitter and proud. She was not sure that the gods themselves might not yield to one who showed that she would not be turned lightly aside.

CHAPTER TWENTY-ONE

THE sun was high when the King came again to the Cave of Words, for he had slept long. But he was now alert and active of mind, his arm having been dressed again, and its pain less. He called by name the ancient councillors of the land, the men, such as Huni, of wrinkled faces and whitened hair, who had been of most power and repute in the peaceful days; and he called also for some, such as Plini and Swashki, younger and more vigorous men, of whom some will come to a nation's front in times of terror and strife, and among these he called Ooli's name, being one whom he would not leave to plot and grumble apart.

"It is vain to call him," Huni said, "he having been slain at this dawn."

"Why," the King exclaimed, "have the apes stirred?" He added, as one ready for wrath: "Was I not to be called, if that should happen before I waked?"

"It was no doing of apes," Huni replied. "Swashki split his skull with a club."

The King thought it might have been a good deed; but he only asked: "Why did he do that?"

"Swashki went to the boats, and he found a loading of gear, and that there were men who took their women aboard. He split Ooli's head, and the men came back, taking off women and gear."

"He did well," the King must admit, when he heard that. "But he should leave such justice to me."

"As to that," Huni replied, being just, and thinking better of Swashki than the King did, "you were not to be waked, except for one cause; and it was a matter that would not wait for a later hour."

"Well it is done," the King said, "and Ooli is little loss. There will be one less to bicker and whine.... You will let the priestess know that I do not ask her to join me now, for I would speak with her quietly apart. I will come to her in the Queen's cave, when this council is through."

He thought that Tela could not improve on that which she had already said, and might do worse, nor did he think it well that she should be seen too often by common men.

When Huni returned, the King had those he had called assembled within the cave, and told them what he had resolved in the night, which was that they must wait, for two days or three, to see whether the apes, having been roused as they had, would quieten if they were left alone. For he allowed, without cavil of words, that they had proved too strong to be expelled from their own land, "though," he must add, "I blame not the gods therefore, but those who were slack to come on the due day, for who can say how the end had been, had we thrust them back from the verge at the first assault?"

Swashki answered to that, in too bold a tone: "We may agree that we wait and watch, for what else is there to do? But I should say that the apes were too many and strong to be overthrown by twice all the men we have, or perhaps twice that again."

His words had the respect of those who knew that he had outfought the apes for his part, and that he had withstood those who would have fled in the night. They would all thank him for that, except those who were crowding on board, for the boats were not enough to have taken all, and those who would have been left would have been in a worse case than they now were.

"We will waste no words," the King said, in a cold tone, "on that which might or might not have been, having to think of that which now is. If the apes have not had enough, they must clamber down to engage us here, for which we must be alert, both by night and day, but if the hours pass, and it shall seem that we are safe from that, I will call you again, and uncover another plan."

Swashki felt that the King's word was a rebuke, which he had swelled too big to endure. He turned to Plini to ask: "Said I not right as to the strength which the apes have?"

Plini looked at him in a considering way: "It is the King's will, as to that, that we say no more."

"Yet," Swashki must persist, "it is that which we all know."

Plini made no reply, and it seemed that the words did not reach the King, who broke up the debate, after he had made some dispositions for watching the apes, and marshalling the strength of the land if there should be invasion in force, such as they must repulse, or all die. Swashki got command of the long beach where the flat-bottomed boats were anchored or laid ashore, for which he asked in a bold way, and which the King could not deny, seeing the part he had played. Ooli came into the talk at this time, and there was one who recalled Tela's words of the night before, that it was the faint of heart who might be nearest to death. They thought she had foreseen more than she had.

Plini walked out at Swashki's side, and, for once, he was the quicker to speak. He said:

"You gave the priestess much praise when you let the air into Ooli's skull. Now I wonder why you did that."

Swashki felt he was mocked, as one whose acts did not look far nor very clearly ahead, but he could not think of a good reply. He could not say aloud that he had been wroth with Ooli because he had made a bungling attempt at his own plan. He had been resolving a plot by which he would put to sea with as many as the boats would contain while taking enough gear, and leave those who stood by the King for the apes to tear. He would become king of a new race in a new land. But it had seemed that Ooli would forestall him in that, and if the man had thought that he would be second to him—well, he had learned better by now....

Bwene thought that he had come off as well as a king can expect to do when his plans fail, so that there is peril for those he rules. He thought that the most danger was past, though there might still be murmurs behind his back. Plini would have been less sure about that, for though he said little, he had heard more than a king is ever likely to do.

Still, had the apes let them alone, the King might have had no cause to doubt his own guess, but he had scarcely gone to the Queen's cave, and was praising Tela for what she had said the night before, when there was outcry that called him forth.

There had been men sent to relieve those who had been stationed to watch the river path above Tela's cave, and they had come back, saying that they had found them in the right place, but they were all dead.

CHAPTER TWENTY-TWO

THE men who had been set to prevent surprise by the river path, and to resist approach to the Sacred Cave, may not have thought that they were asked to take more than the common hazard of war. Their orders were to send back one who could run with speed, if they should be attacked, or if they should see any sign that the apes were astir. They had but a narrow front, and they were to fall back if they were pressed, taking as much time as they could, and knowing that relief would be advancing toward their rear.

That they sent no word of their need may be held for proof that they were taken by swift surprise, and it is a likely guess that the apes used the river to wade or swim, and cut them off from all help at the first attack, which may have been in the night.

The sure thing was that they were all dead, and that they had lacked the power or the will to retire from the place which they first held. They lay in a close heap, and their bodies had been drained of the living blood, as it was the apes' habit to do.

The King saw that he could not place such an outpost again, being so far from support. The river path must be given up. He said to Tela that she must abandon the Sacred Cave. Let her stay with the Queen till this peril had left the land, or they themselves should be sped or gone, which might seem the more likely end. She agreed to that, though she thought that she might have found safety in the deep caves, where the apes would not have found it easy to come. She was glad to think that she had hidden much which she would be loath to lose, and yet more for it to come to other hands than her own.

There was strife of tongues as to whether this exploit of the apes made it more likely or less that they would attempt to invade the land. Some took it to be no less than a gesture of war, showing the greater things that they were preparing to do: others said it showed that they would attack any party that might be far from support, but that they would not venture to try their strength against the whole nation of men in their own land.

They took comfort from the evident fact that the apes had retired from the verge of the seaward cliffs, where they could no longer be seen by those who looked up from below. Men judged in this more by themselves than by the evidence of the meagre facts, showing their own valour or weakness of heart, or what they would have been likely to do in a kindred case. It was a mere guess.

It was one, also, which was not left long in debate, for on the next day the apes came.... But before that there had been further council called, and some things resolved, and one done.

Bwene called the chiefs of the people back at once to the Cave of Words, seeing that the apes had become an active menace, which could not be ignored, and that it was desirable that those who led should speak with a single voice, and should be clear in their own minds as to what was purposed to do. His arm was quiet now, and the fever stayed. He did not wait for other voices to rise, but spoke at once, showing his thoughts as he had not done till that hour.

"There are some," he said, "who have murmured in the last days, saying that we have stirred a foe that we cannot face, and that they have been led in the wrong way, whether by my own fault, or the counsel of wrathful gods.

"I will not say they lack cause, either for discontent or for fear, nor do I say that the gods have not scourged our land, seeing the disease by which we have sickened, and many die. Nor will I debate of whether we might not have walked at will in the apes' land at this hour, had there been none who was slack to join the assault we made. We have enough matter for thought, without contention for that which is done, and we cannot change.

"But I will remind you of this, that we have not come to wreck from a summer sea. We were in tempest before, from which we were like to sink if we did not turn our oars to a new course.

"The way we tried was not good. You may say that now, if you will. But was there a better to have preferred? And, if so, is it not still to be tried?

"Now the choices we have, as I see them, are these, and no more.

"We may stay here, waiting the apes' attack. They may come, and prevail, eating us out of the land, which will be the end of the race of men. Or they may be thrown back, or may not attack us at all, but where are we then? We were agreed before that it has become death to stay in this land, it having bred a sickness we cannot cure. So we may put aside this doubt of what the apes may be likely to do, seeing that we should be gone, whether they will be coming or no. If we look deep, we may call them the direct mercy of gods, urging us to be gone, which we might else have lacked vigour to do.

"Where then can we go? There is the way of the sea, to which some have cast eyes in this urgent need, though it had not been counselled in quieter days. We could not all go by that way, for the boats would be far too few, even though we should take little of water and food, and less gear. We do not know to where we should steer, nor on what hostile coast we might land, even if we should not drift on an endless sea, such as must boil at last in the sun's pit.... We should be free of our troubles here, even as we pushed off from the land, but for what others we should exchange we know less.

"Then there is the land of the Ho-Tus. They are men, much as ourselves, but they are much larger than we. That we could conquer their land I have never thought, nor that they would show us any goodwill. But they might give us passage through without strife, if they should be rightly approached, and some payment made. That may be asked at no loss, even though they reject our plea.

"But in these last days I have pondered another plan. There is the secret way through the caves, which the priestess knows, by which the upper land was invaded before. If we should go by that way again, seeking passage rather than strife, it may be that we could be far across the land of the apes, even before they should be aware, and while the night would be a cloak to conceal that which we were attempting to do.

"Now I have skinned my own mind in the sight of all. I would have any speak who can give us a better plan."

The King ceased, and was followed by a confusion of words, amid which Swashki was silent for once, thinking that all went in the way he would. There was much said of dangers and doubts, and of how houses and gear must be left, such as could not be borne away either by sea or land, but there was none who put forward a better plan, finding it simpler to carp at those which came from the King.

It was late before Plini spoke, not so much because he had nothing to say, as because he was in no haste to be heard; but he said at last, when there came a pause in the words of those who had thought less: "The land of the apes extends far to the north, but it could be crossed in a shorter time. There are mountains eastward that can be seen."

"You think," the King asked, "that it could be done?"

Plini was cautious in his reply: "It could be tried. The mountains might not be easy to scale, nor do we know what is beyond.... We might live where the apes would die.... We should be many hours filing out of the caves, and before we could be placed in the best array.... The apes may lie in the canyons during the night, and the plain be bare.... There would not be much we could bear away by that path, having to link hands through the dark.... It could be tried; for a poor hope must be better than none."

He spoke resolutely, though his words were not of a sanguine sound, and so made the plan good to those whose fortitude was not less than his own, and their judgment sober alike.

There was one who said: "It would be a great curse, if we should be attacked on so long a march, that our women are many more than ourselves, and that they do not fight as those of the apes do."

"They would have to fight," the King said, "to the best they could, having their lives for stake."

"As to that," Swashki said, "we must face the fact: There are women now who outnumber our need, whether we take the perils of land or sea. We should choose the best, and I should say that every man should have one at his side, and also a girl who is partly grown; but, for the rest, they must shift as themselves can.

"I do not choose the way of the land; but, if I did, I should say that the use of some would be for the apes to eat, while those of more worth would win free."

It was a sign of the desperation of the position of which men were aware that these words were received with silence, if not assent.

Only there was one who said, whether of charity or that he had a frugal mind would be hard to tell: "They could bear gear, as some must, for those who fight should have their hands free."

The King said: "I have allowed talk without stint, and it seems that none has a better plan. I have a mind to give all men choice, that we go in two ways, and those who will may take to the boats, and those who prefer the land may follow where I shall lead, for that way will be mine. But before we decide that, we will first approach the Ho-Tus. For if they will let us pass, it may be the better for all, and we shall need the boats to get our folk over the great river that few could swim.

"Now I must choose someone who has skill of discourse and assurance of front, to do our errand to the Ho-Tu King, and I will name Swashki for that."

Swashki had looked pleased at the first part of this speech, seeing that he was likely to find that for which he schemed put into his hand without more trouble for him. He did not doubt that he could persuade enough to go by the boats, nor that he would be leader of them. But he had no will to be sent to the Ho-Tu King. It was a mission, he said, with a humility of which he had shown little during the last week, which he did not feel equal to undertake.

"And why not?" the King asked. "You are a man not backward of speech. You did not protest that you were not equal to undertake the command, when I made you leader of those who climbed up the cliff of thorns, nor did I have occasion to blame that which you did; and you were efficient to do your part (if not more) when Ooli was slain."

"But this," Swashki replied, "is a task of another kind. How could I talk, not knowing the Ho-Tu tongue?"

"As to that," the King asked, "is there one who does?"

"Yet there may be those who would make better shift to overcome that defect, which I have no cunning to do."

"Oh," the King said, "but I think you have; and this is for me to decide. I give honour to whom I will. You are bold of manner, which one should be who is to stand up to the Ho-Tu King, and you are of a good aspect, and nimble of mind."

"I should say," Swashki replied (and it was at least certain that he had not too much respect for his own king, however he might have faced him of the Ho-Tus), "that it is women's work, of whom we have plenty to spare, for they are seldom wanting of words."

"It is idle," the King answered, showing displeasure at that, "to propose that which would be a slight to the Ho-Tus, as they would have wit to see; for it would defeat its own end."

"There would be no slight," Swashki persisted, "if those who should go would be of most esteem in the land. Let the priestess go."

"The Priestess," the King replied, "is not to be ordered thus, even by me. Nor do prudent men jeopardize that which is of most value to them."

There were two things here at which Swashki was not pleased. He saw that the King, in his heart, considered the mission to be of a dangerous sort, which confirmed a doubt in his own mind, and he liked it no better for that; also, he saw that the King regarded Tela as being too precious to be so risked, but that he himself would have been a lighter matter to lose, and his values would have been put the opposite way.

He might have shown temper at this, in his shallow pride, and roused the wrath of the King more than he had yet done, but there was one who said: "It is the goddess should help us here. She should know tongues. For what did she come, but for such a need?"

The King and Swashki came to an accord here which they did not guess. The King said, in a voice to silence any who might be of a diverse mind: "There shall no woman be sent. Nor will I send one who says himself that he is too lacking in wit. Huni shall go, and two others besides, so that they may take counsel if the Ho-Tus should offer some bargain which we do not foresee. They shall have full power, even to pledge my own word; for Huni is one I have learned to trust, and I would have this arranged, if it may be, without hindrance of long debate."

Huni may have been no better pleased to hear this than Swashki had been before, but he said less. That may have been because his thoughts were less on his own gain, and more on the King's will, or merely that he was of a spirit too mean to resist that which he was ordered to do.

CHAPTER TWENTY-THREE

HUNI set out early next morning with two companions of age and dignity akin to his own. They crossed the great river in a shallow skiff, finding it a sore trouble to keep its course against the current, which was strong at that hour, with an outward tide. They might have had rowers with better muscles than theirs, but it was their design to moor the skiff on the further bank, so that it would be ready for their return.

They hoped to cross unobserved, so that none would see where the skiff lay, and so they thought they had done. They looked up a wide river, which they could see for two miles, or perhaps more, to where it curved out of view. On the right bank, there was the high cliff that rose to the plateau where the apes dwelt, and on the left, being the southern shore, was a lower land that was tall only with trees, which rose, dense and high, to the very edge of the flood. But it appeared all to be empty of life of a better kind—or of a worse, if we will.

They tied up the skiff, with sufficient slackness of rope, in a place where they could find it again, being beneath a bush which overhung the water at any tide, and that was bright with a scarlet flower. They made slow way through a wilderness tangle of briars, till they came to a path that was narrow, but trodden well. They followed this for a time, and came to a place where two huts stood in a cleared space.

They were not large, but very solidly built, being in a land where timber was of no value at all. Huni looked at them with respect, coming from a land where wood was not easy to find, and the best they had was that which would drift down the river at some times of year, and be cast ashore at the next tide. The huts were closed and silent, and they thought it would be prudent to leave them alone, to which most men would agree; but while they stood there, debating what manner of skins had been used to over-cover the roofs, a man came from among the trees, and looked at them in a very natural surprise.

He was very largely made, and of more than eight cubits in height His skin was blue-black, glossy and smooth. His hair was short and black, and cut into a pattern upon his head. He wore a blouse and tunic of some yellow silk-like stuff which was not over-clean, for he was a man of a common kind, who had been working within the woods. His hands were empty. As he looked, surprise gave way to amusement, as though that which he saw was a joke he would have been sorry to miss.

He spoke to them, and when he realised that he was not under-stood, he chuckled, as though the joke grew. Huni tried his own tongue, and the giant wagged his head, laughing aloud.

Huni resorted to signs, which he had expected to have to use, and which he had thought out in advance. The man appeared to un-derstand better, though he was not tickled the less. In the end, he waved a huge hand, pointing to them to continue along the path, and came with them, so that they supposed that they would be guided to the King, for whom they had asked.

They went on thus for about two hours, at a pace which it was not easy for them to hold, but while the giant appeared to regard them in a friendly rather than a menacing way, it was free from any element of respect, and he made it plain from the first that he meant his pace to be theirs, lifting Huni with a great kick from behind, when he showed a disposition to lag. It was a kick that was not the less hard because it was given with a laugh as great as itself, and after that he had but to move to the rear to cause the three to break into a trot in which each was reluctant to be the last.

They went thus along a path which was closed in by a dense-ness of jungle on either side, till they came to a place of felling of trees, where there were a score of men at work with stone axes and other tools, who paused to stare at the procession which came out from the wood.

They all seemed to be of a jovial mood, except that one, who seemed to be a foreman over the rest, questioned their guide—or driver might be a better word—in a more sober way; but the talk seemed to end in a jest with him too. Yet it was easy for Huni to un-derstand that what was a jest to them might be other to his compan-ions and him, when leather thongs were fetched, by which their wrists were bound to each other, more tightly than it was pleasant to feel. Huni had a companion tied on each side, so that his hands were secure, but each of the others had a hand free by which they could have released all, but it was not a thing which it might be prudent to try, being surrounded by these men who were twice their size, besides that they were of fewer years, being workmen in the vigour of youth. They took their bonds in a quiet way, though with some gestures of protest, and words of which they hoped that the tone would be understood, if it could not go beyond that.

They having been so secured, their drover started forward again, the woodsmen resuming their toil with laughter and jesting among themselves.

Huni saw that the thongs were meant for no more than to provide that they should not run different ways, when two of them might have been hard for the blue-black giant to catch; but he may be excused if he wished that it were Swashki who trotted along that path, with breath which was now coming in painful jerks, as he strove to avert the risk of another kick.

But it seemed that their drover saw their condition, and had no wish to cause them distress, for he slackened his pace, so that they could walk according to the length of their own legs, and they took what comfort they could from that. Though it was no more than a man might do who drove pigs, and wished to get them to market in such condition that the butcher could not find excuse to abate his price.

They went on till the sun was low in the western sky, having no more than a short rest, when they came to an unbridged stream that they must wade waist-deep to cross. They drank here, and Huni's companions using their free hands to draw out food from the store which was in the satchels upon their backs, their driver made no motion of protest when they sat down on the bank to eat.

Then they went on again, meeting at times more of the Ho-Tus, to whom their coming must be explained anew, and always in the tone of a tickling jest. There were more buildings around them now, and much else at which Huni would have looked with lively eyes, but that he was too tired of limb and apprehensive of mind to care for aught but the length of road that might still be stretching ahead, and that which he must not fail to explain when he should come at last to the King.

What he did come to at last was a wooden gate, and whether it were that of the King's house was a thing he was not destined to know.

CHAPTER TWENTY-FOUR

THROUGH the upright bars of the gate, Huni saw a winding path that was gardened with care, and its sides were brilliant with flowering shrubs. Their guide sat down on the ground outside the gate, and gave them an urgent motion to do the same, to which they did not object. Then he raised his voice in a shrill cry, somewhat like a sea-bird's wail, and being one that would carry far.

But it seemed that he could have been heard on a lower note, for almost at once a man, who must have been walking in the garden, came out from a side path, and approached the gate. He was the largest of the Ho-Tus that Huni had yet seen, being tallest, and much the greatest in bulk, and there was some dignity in his gait, and in the tones of his voice, as of one used to command, though he had the merry eyes, and the quickness to see a jest, which seemed to be common to all his race.

He asked a brief question now, and opened the gate, turning his head at the same time to shout backward a curt command, with little raising of voice, as to those whom he knew to be near at hand.

Huni and his companions would have risen out of respect to they knew not whom, but it is not a thing to be quickly done by three men who are tied in one string, and, as they swayed about, their guide jerked them down with a powerful hand, at which the curiosity in the great man's eyes gave way to the twinkle of one who enjoyed the jest.

Huni was quick to see that it must be a mark of respect to sit in this land, and he thought that he would not repeat the mistake, which indeed, as the event proved, he had no occasion to do. But he was vexed in another way, not seeing how he could talk the language of signs with his wrists tied as they were, at which thought he took the bold course of asking his comrades to loose him on either side, which they proceeded to do.

Meanwhile there was a running of naked feet down the garden path, and a woman came, bearing a low stool, very strongly made, as was needed for the burden it had to bear. This was the first woman whom they had seen in the Ho-Tu land, and they looked at her with the greatest surprise they had yet felt, for she was not more than half the size of the men, of the same blue-black colour, soft and rounded and plump; and though the men were all fully clothed, she was quite bare.

They had not known that such was the custom in the land of the Ho-Tus, concerning which, had the black giants been asked, they would have exclaimed in surprise: "What! Would you clothe beasts?" But, in fact, there was none to ask, for the Ho-Tus were their own law, and none would come to that land with a questioning tongue.

The Chief (for he was much less than the King, who was two days' journey away) sat down on the stool, as his custom was when he did justice outside his gate, and, as he did so, half a score of his wives came running out, and gathered round him, or played quietly about, as their humour was. They were a merry curious group, all as bare as she who had first come, and he gave them no more regard than had they been kittens around his feet.

"What," he asked, "have you caught here?"

Huni understood that their guide was narrating how they had appeared to him, and how he had brought them there, though the words were foreign to him; and after that the Chief asked two questions, which were shortly answered, and then he looked at Huni as at one whose time had come, if there should be aught that he wished to say.

Huni did not know whether he had yet come to the King, but he saw that it would be a better mistake to give that place to a lesser man, than to put a king low; and, in any case, he could do little but to explain, by the gestures he had rehearsed, the peril in which his country stood, and the favour he came to plead.

This he did, perhaps as well as a man might, and he had a sure belief that he was well understood, though he did not get much comfort from that, for it seemed that he was a better jest than he had been at the first. The Chief let him go on for as long as he would, talking the language of signs, and seemed to give a good heed, though he made no reply; for when he spoke, as he did at times, he would look at their guide; and after that he spoke, in a general way, to the wives that were round his feet.

Huni felt that his request was not being received in the right way, and could he have understood all that was said he would have known that he had made a good guess.

"You have more travel to do," the Chief had said, "for it seems that there is some sport to be had, of which I must let others know, lest I lose friends." He told the man to go at once to two chiefs, whose homes were not more than a day's journey away. He said: "You will tell them that if they choose they can join me here, within two days from now, with all the men they can call, and bringing spears of the larger size. Tell them there may be apes to catch, without the trouble of climbing a cliff which we do not love.... When you come back, there may be a joint for your own dish." He waved his hand, and the man went.

Huni wondered what would happen if they should rise and run. Would the burly chief scamper after, in a clumsy, panting pursuit? Would they be chased by the litter of laughing wives? It seemed that the chance was theirs, but it was one that he had no purpose to try. He was come with a mission which flight would not help, and he must not assume that it would fail because the ways of these people were not easy to understand.

There was something also, if not of menace, of assured strength, in the fact that they were treated in this casual way, and that the Ho-Tus appeared to bear no weapons of any kind. But he had little space to debate such thoughts, for the Chief rose, and was beside them in two strides, his wives frisking around his heels.

He grasped Huni under the arm, to do which he must bend low, and pulled him to his feet, at which his companions rose also. He turned Huni round, looking at him with amusement that touched contempt. He spoke down to his wives, as one who addresses a herd.

"It seems," he said, "that we have done well to feed in the fatter lands.... You will put them in the pens for this time, and there they may stay, if they fatten well, till I will tell you again.... But if they will not eat as you think they should, they must be slaughtered to-morrow night." He added kindly: "If you have to do that, they should be handled with care, lest they do any of you a hurt, and you should come to the same end, which I should be sorry to see."

The wives laughed at that, seeing that they had got a benign lord, and one with whom it was a good guess that their lives would be merry and long; yet the warning was not a jest, for should one of them come to be badly hurt when they would be preparing these men for the pot, it would have been to the Chief's table that she would have been likely to go, and not as one who eats at the side. For the Ho-Tus had a hatred of waste, and, most of all, of the waste of food, when it is juicy and good.

The Chief turned Huni round, still having a grasp of his arm from which he would have had a poor hope to break free. He pointed to a joint which, he said, must be for his own dish; but the most, he said, would be more fit for the kitchen plates.

"You can call the dogs," he said, "lest they run when they see where we will have them to be." He turned away, and went in, a wife picking up the stool, and bearing it back by the same way, closing the gate as she went through.

Huni and his companions had some surprise to find themselves in the midst of a group of the Ho-Tu women, who were of less size than themselves, and seemed to be in a merry mood; as they might well be, being pleased with the prizes which came their way. One of them whistled twice, and a pack of dogs, six in number, and somewhat larger than wolves, came running from round the fence.

Huni and his companions became easy to drive; for, when they looked at the dogs, they decided that they would rather be pushed by the women's hands than have the dogs' teeth snapping about their calves.

CHAPTER TWENTY-FIVE

RAINA, finding herself a somewhat superfluous resident in the Queen's cave, and having more time for thought than her comfort required, was disposed to doubt, not for the first time or the second, whether she had come to a good place.... However that might be, Raina saw that she had come to a place where she was not a success. Whether as woman or goddess, she could not feel that she was greatly required.

She had not felt quite the same while she had been Tela's companion in the solitude of the Sacred Cave. Slowly, they had been approaching one another across the gap of dividing language and race to a common friendship. But now Tela would talk to Bira in an intimacy in which Raina must feel that she had no part.... She had an idea that she could be Swashki's fourth wife if she would, but it was not a prospect for which she would sell her soul, and call it a fair deal.

It was a world that did not appear to need, though it had come to tolerate her; and had placed her in a position which it had now become too preoccupied with its own ills to further regard. For it was a world of which the foundations swayed. If its eyes should be turned upon her as a possible cause, it might be her death in a choice of unpleasant ways; or, at the best, it might be much the same in the end, for she saw it as a world that was near its fall.

These were her thoughts on the morning when Huni left in search of the Ho-Tu King. Till he should return, it was understood that all plans were stayed—to be brought, one or more, to prompt resolve, when it should be known whether there would be freedom to cross the Ho-Tu land. But, whatever might be in doubt, it was common to every mind that a new country was to be sought, whether by land or sea, whether by single or diverse ways, so that men turned over the precious things that were theirs, making exchanges in which the more portable goods rose to fantastic relative values, and made impossible plans as to how much they would bear away.

And as the hours of the morning passed, Swashki might be observed to have become active in preparing the boats for sea, which was a matter the King might have rebuked as being beyond any decision which he had made until Huni should have returned. But Bwene would not seem to see even as much as he did. He was content to watch, and to wait what the occasion would require at its own time. So Swashki had the water tanks filled to the brim, and stores of food of the more lasting kinds carried aboard, and of all manner of things such as men will require when they come to a new land. He got around him a group of those who thought him leader enough, reminding them that the King had said that he would hold to the land, so that they must shift for themselves, if they should resolve that the sea might be the less perilous way, and he began to talk as one who would make his own laws as to who should come, and what women and children should be allowed, as though he were already king of a sea-borne fleet.

Thus it was, at about two hours after noon, when word was brought to the King that the apes were assembling on the height of the seaward cliffs, and this he had scarcely heard, when there was another call that the apes had come down the river path, and were attacking those who had been stationed in force at its lower end.

They had not delayed their attack during the last days from any doubt of their strength to destroy those who had been left alone till their own folly exposed a weakness which the apes had been slow to guess. In fact, since the post which had been placed on the river path had been destroyed without any loss to them, they had supposed their human foes to be weaker and less of courage than they actually were.

They had delayed a general invasion of the lower land only until the whole nation of apes might be assembled for the taking of equal spoil. They came to hunt, not to die. They may have lacked wit to perceive that men would fight harder for the greater peril which battered against their doors, and the more so if there were no place to which they could hope to flee.

Bwene saw that, and was discontent with himself that the lading of the boats had not been more closely controlled. He would not have men facing the apes with a backward thought of a beach where some, if not all, might find escape from the present foe. Had he known that the attack would come on this day—but he had no time to think of what might have been. He sent Plini with strong support for those who fought to keep closed the mouth of the river path. He said he would go himself to take command of those who must meet what he supposed would be the main army of apes at the foot of the seaward cliffs. He sent one he could trust to Swashki, ordering him to come himself the same way, with the best men that were at his call, leaving women and such as were old or weak to continue the garnishing of the boats. He judged that Swashki would provide for that work to go on, whatever order he might receive, so that it was best it should come from him.

Had the coming of the apes been delayed till the next day, it may not be unjust to Swashki, seeing what was to happen then, to conclude that he would not have scrupled to gather his friends on board, and sail away, leaving those for whom the boats were too small to defend themselves or to die, as they might be best able to do.

But he could not do that now, except at some added peril, and loss of much which should be taken on board, for his preparations were not complete. And so, while he debated with himself what he should do, the order came from the King, which could not be denied, except it were in a public way, for which he found courage of decision less than enough.

So he made the King's orders his, and having provided that the work of loading the boats should not slacken, he went to the support of those who fought in a battle which did not go so ill at the first as it might be thought that it would be likely to do.

For as to the mouth of the river path, there had been digging there of a great pit, where its width was not much, and when this had been hollowed out to a depth of many feet, and a breadth which it had been supposed that no ape could cross, the river had been let in, so that the effect was that the water spread at this point to the wall of rock; and the earth which had been thrown out was piled into a high mound, from behind which men could look out with better heart than if they had faced their foes on an open field.

The apes came to the ditch, and stopped in a snarling way, all the path behind, so far as it could be seen for the river's twists, being crowded by those who pressed on behind for a share of the coming spoil. The men shouted loud, and threw spears, such as they used for the killing of seals. These had a long thong attached, by which they could be recovered again, and were not meant to be thrown far. They did little hurt to the apes, by whom they were seized, and the thongs jerked from the throwers' hands, so that this sport was soon done.

The apes did not stand long in delay after there had been some shrill debating among themselves. Several males that were the largest among them leapt over the width of the ditch, even to the high level of the mound. It was such a leap as the men had not thought it possible that they would attempt, yet there was only one who fell short, and he came to no hurt, falling into the water with a loud splash and swimming out to the river, where a swarm of his companions were already heading, so that they should pass the mound, and land on the bank below.

The apes that had gained the mound fought fiercely with teeth and hands, but they were few to the swarm of men by whom they were met, and one, and then another, were forced back, so that they fell to the water punctured by many spears, and sank where they fell; and those who swam round must find it a harder thing to clamber banks which were crowded by eager foes, than it had been to throw them back from the seaward cliffs, when it had been the men by whom the climbing was done.

It can be told in few words that the apes could not prevail at this point, and when darkness came Plini was able to send word to the King that he had held his ground, though with loss more than enough, and that the apes had retired, as he thought, for the last time.

At the seaward cliffs, the fight had been maintained at a more difficult cost, and with less reason to boast when the darkness fell. For a time, the apes had been met as they came clambering and sliding down the cliff side, and each had been overwhelmed by the crowd of men who were waiting at the foot. The first had died, and those who followed had paused thereat, till there should be many who could make the last leap at once.

The men held their own after that for a time along the base of the cliff, which became a shambles of blood and death. The apes were more than a match for a single man, though they had few weapons, except that here and there was a spear of the hard wood of the trees which grew in the gorges above. But the men pressed upon them from all sides as they came down to the level land, battering them with clubs, and stabbing with fish-bone spears, so that they must each strive for himself, and could not make a good front of array.

And when men had been driven somewhat back, and there were those who looked up with a fainting of heart, seeing that all the side of the cliffs was black with descending apes, there was a shout of new hope, and a forward rush, with the coming of Swashki, and those he led.

Then the fight swayed back to the very foot of the cliff, and though it receded again, and men were driven by a tide that would not return, yet that was not till the dusk was near; and though the apes had won some ground, they must be content with no more for that day, and its cost to them had exceeded that which they had supposed needful to pay for every man that the land held.

CHAPTER TWENTY-SIX

SWASHKI might have been excused had he slept after a hard day. But, in fact, he planned. He had the vigour of mature youth. The sickness which had weakened or destroyed his fellows had passed him by. He did not tire himself with abstruse thought. He had desires, and his mind would stir itself for their gratification, but did not exceed that necessity. So far, it had been able to gratify them without being overworked. This crisis of strife and projected flight was a harder test, but he would have said (with some appearance of support from the facts) that it had but lifted him to his natural place, where he moved with as much ease as before. He had advantage over most of his race, in that his mind was not hindered by complexities of doubt, or of ideals, or contending desires. He knew what he would have, and he went for it by the shortest path.

He looked at the present strait, and its issues were as simple and clear as any his life had known. He saw that the apes had been held back for one afternoon, but he had looked at the swarming numbers which formed their rear, and he had decided that there could be only one end, which he did not purpose to share. As to the King's plan of escaping by the way of the caves, and slipping off in the night behind the rear of the apes, he thought its dangers to be greater than those of the sea, which he preferred, for it was more familiar to him, whether as friend or foe. Besides, he did not intend to be one subordinate to the King, such as he could break with a word, having had a better idea.

In any case, what was the use of thinking of that escape, when the approach to the Sacred Cave was in the hands of their foes? Or to wait for Huni's return, when the apes had already overrun the way to the Great River, from the cliff foot to the sea?

There was one sane thing for him to do, and that was to escape in time to be clear of the fighting which must come with the morrow's dawn. This was not as simple as he would have liked it to be, though he was not embarrassed by any loyalty, either to his King or his fellow men, finding it trouble enough to make his own comfort sure. But the boats were many; and the selection of those men he would take aboard and the provision of what they should be required or allowed to bring off, were not matters which could be completed secretly, nor in an hour's time.

He saw also that, if the boats should lie at the quays (at which there was space for less than a tenth of those that were now at home), or be pulled up on the shore, when men should become aware of final defeat, there might be a panic rush for safety which could be found in no other way, such as would cause them to be put off overfilled with a muddled crowd, in excess of those for whom provision would have been made, and including some that he would have been sorry to have. Even the King might be among those who would come on board at the last, and his whole plan shake at the root.

Having weighed these facts, he decided that it would be better to sail with a smaller fleet than to risk all by attempting more. He sent for those he had entrusted with the garnishing of the boats, and enquired how much they had been able to do. He gave instructions that men should not cease their labour during the night, and he allocated crews to as many boats as would be ready to sail at the dawn, telling them that they must be prepared to be instantly called, whether by night or day, though he did not say when it would be, with such women as he would allow them to bring, and at peril of being left if they should be slack when the signal came.

He meant to sail within two hours of when the sun should appear, and, having made his dispositions for this, Swashki of the Three Wives turned his thoughts to an affair of his own, which he did not intend to fail.

The three wives were well enough, and he had no complaint against them. But to be overburdened with women is a mistake for those who go by the sea's ways, which he did not intend, either for himself or for those he led. This was a crisis at which his wives must shift for themselves, and if they should come to an ape's teeth, he supposed it would be a thing he would never know, which was the more comfortable way. He thought that one wife must now be enough, and he would have the best he had seen (as was his custom in all he did), and that would be the goddess, as she was called (but he cared nothing for that, she being a woman beyond dispute), whom he had desired in the Sacred Cave, and again when she had gone with him by the Cliff of Thorns on the next day. He did not consider what her own feelings might be, having most concern for his own, but he supposed himself to be one whom a woman of sense would not find it hard to admire.

Had he put Raina out of his thoughts, and made a choice from the wives he already had, he might have brought his affairs to a different end, but women have confused the course of human events at all times, from when they first discovered the guile of dress, as they may do to the last days.

As the sun showed over the cliff wall, he took ten men he could trust, being of those who had served on his own boat, and who were used to take their orders from him, and made his way to the Queen's cave, a distance of two miles, or perhaps more.

The Queen's cave was not closed by a narrow hole, as was that of the King, but was secure in another way. There was a lower cave, which was open to all who would, being no more than a wide-mouthed cavity in the side of the cliff; but high up in its sidewall there was a slit which gave access to caves on a higher plane. Up to this slit there had been cut rough steps in the rock, which could not be ascended except by those in a single file, and that not with an easy speed, while at the head of these steps there was a stone, large and lightly balanced, which could be overturned at a child's touch, to the destruction of those who might not be desired for a closer view. And it was the law that this stone should be overset upon any who should ascend till they had called at the foot, and had the Queen's consent to go up.

Inside, the cave was spacious and high, and had some daylight from clefts in the outer wall, which were yet not of a size to be source of danger to those within, even had they been accessible from below. The cave was not of one chamber alone, but had others beyond, as well as passages opening backwards into the hills, of which the Queen may have known more than she would be quick to tell.

It was clear that the Queen's cave was not to be lightly entered by any man of the tribe, and even in the confusion of these days Swashki tried a bold throw, but he was at a pass which he felt could best be overcome by decision and speed, at which, indeed, he was more adept than at the using of subtler ways.

He stood at the foot of the stairs, and cried: "Queen, may I come up? I have a word from the King."

There was a moment's delay, and a sound of voices within the cave, and then the Queen herself appeared overhead. She said: "You may come up." And then, as he began to ascend, and the ten men at his heels, "but those you bring can remain below."

That was not how he had meant it to be, but it was not an order safe to dispute, with the Queen's hand resting lightly upon the stone, and he already upon the stair. He thought: "When I am there, it will be but a moment to guard the stone, and I can call them up to my side, or I can overset it myself while they stand safely away, and its threat will cease." He was not diffident of himself, nor of his power to bring his affairs to a good end.

But the Queen did not step back. She stepped sideward to let him pass, or to see into the cave, and as he did so, he looked into the face of the King.

Even Swashki must have a moment of confusion at that, remembering what he had called aloud a moment before. He might have drawn back, but it was clear that it was not a thing which it would have been wisdom to do.

In the next instant he had regained the assurance that was more easy to him than to one who was more sensitive to surrounding minds.

"King," he said, "I have prepared boats, in which, if you will, the Queen can be placed with more safety than she can have here, and I have been bold to use your name, that I might come up and tell you what I have done in a quiet way, for I had heard you were here."

He gave circumstance to a ready lie, when he added: "I have brought men of trust, who could be her guard if you should wish her to go."

"The Queen," Bwene replied, "will prefer to stay here. But you have come at a good time, for we have just been talking of you."

Whether he believed the tale he had heard, could not have been guessed by a wiser man than Swashki was ever likely to be.

The King had been awake and active for as long as Swashki himself, though he was more burdened with years, and his thoughts had been more of others, and less of what he might be able to do for his own good. He had learnt that the dispositions of the apes were not of an instant menace, though they were ominous of evil to be, and he had come here to consult with Bira and her companions within the cave, and to tell the plans that he had resolved during the night.

He had said, before Swashki came: "The apes do not seem likely to vex us in the next hour. They did not come down in greater force during the night, but rather withdrew some of those who had descended before. But they are gathering on the cliff tops in a strength which is dreadful to see; and, as I suppose, they will come upon us in force at a later hour, such as we shall not lightly endure.

124

"Yet, for this day, I am resolved that so it must be, for there is no retreat, or at least not for the number that we still are; but if the day pass, and Huni do not return (and he may have trouble enough to get past the apes, even if he be back with a good word), then I purpose, as darkness comes, to try the plan I have spoken before, that is to retreat by way of the Sacred Cave.

"For since the apes were yesterday repulsed at the river path, there is report that they have retired from that side, which is likely enough, as they may come down, as much as they may desire, by the other way. They may keep a watch at the Cliff of Thorns, but that will be no vexation to us, for we shall have no occasion to go so far. We may enter the Sacred Cave under cover of night, being seen of none, and the more apes that are down here, the less there will be overhead to dispute our way.... I came to ask," he turned to Tela to say, "is the way hard to take, in the darkness, for those who are old or weak, or for the young, or such as must be burdened with gear? For we must not go naked of all, if we can contrive in a better way."

He asked this, having care for all, as a king should. He did not think to leave half the women, or children too weak to run, for the apes to tear, as Swashki would plan to do, though he could resolve in a cool mind that they must endure to be slaughtered during the day, so that the time of escape could be chosen well.

Tela told him all that she could. She did not question the plan, knowing that the King was better able than she to weigh the chances of flight or strife, but it was plain that it was not a way to take if there were a better choice to be had. She asked: "Can we endure them during the day, their number being so great?"

"We can do that which we must. I have a mind to attack them before they are fully ready for us, which is more, I think, than they will expect us to do. I think we may cut off a part of the apes which are in the houses toward the shore, and if we can do that, they may be in a less insolent mood for the later hours of the day.... I think to send Swashki on that command, for he is a bold and confident man, and yet, if he fall, as I think he may, there are few I would more willingly spare. Also, it will take his mind off the boats, on which it dwells more than it should while we must still set face to a most pitiless foe.... When the night comes, those who would take the chance of the sea will be free to choose, as I shall say at the right time, and as far as the number of boats allows."

As he said this, they had heard the voice of Swashki calling beneath, and the King added: "A word from me? Well, that is what he will get. But what is he doing here?"

The Queen asked: "He may come up?"

"He can come, if you will. You need not say I am here. Let him see that for himself.

So the Queen had summoned him to the King's sight.

Swashki heard what the King said, but his concern was not great. He had no wish to take the Queen to the boats. It seemed that it was a lie that had served its use, and that it would be no more trouble to him. That they had been talking about himself seemed a very natural thing. He supposed that most men regarded him now as being one of the first in the land, for so merit is sure to rise when peril is round the door.

He had been active all night, while it seemed that the King could do no more than sit in a woman's cave, though the sun mounted the sky. He could not have said that the King had done less than well on the last day, but now he regarded him in the insolent strength of his own youth, and he looked at a tired man. A month ago, he would have drawn back in fear from the King's eyes, had they been but doubtful in their regard: he would have trembled beneath his frown. But much had happened since then. There had been changes enough, but he supposed that there would be more in the coming day, that being a point on which he was not wrong.

CHAPTER TWENTY-SEVEN

SWASHKI heard the King's words, but his attention was more for Raina than him. His eyes went to her. He saw that the cave contained no more than three women, and one man for whom he supposed he was more than match. It was a position with which he should be able to deal with ease.

The King said: "You can sit. For these are days when all should rest when they can, and I have orders to give."

He sat down himself, as one who had no suspicion of any guile.

Swashki did not respond. He looked round the cave.

"I would speak," he said, "with the goddess, somewhat apart."

It was such a thing as the King had not known since he had come to his present power twenty-two years before, but he showed no sign of resentment or of surprise, watching for the man to reveal himself, in the way that a king must learn. He said: "Well, you can do that."

Raina sat on the sealskin floor, as the way of the women was. She was at Tela's side, and it was clear that she must move if Swashki were to be able to speak to her in a private way. She did not suppose that he would have words she would wish to hear, and her first resolve was to keep her place, and tell him to say what he would there, or else nothing at all. But she considered that his request had the King's assent, and that it was not worth while for there to be trouble from her.

As the King may have done, though he gave no sign, she felt that Swashki's coming had more meaning than he had said, and her mind was alert thereat, seeing that it might be well to learn more of what was hidden within his own.

"I know not why," she said, "we should talk apart," as one who protests against no more than a trivial thing; but as she said it she rose, so that her movement showed the assent on which her words were less clear. She walked to the inner wall of the cave, so that

Swashki must follow, being further from the stair, and with her friends sitting between.

"Goddess," he said, using the title without respect, as though it were no more than a woman's name, "the Queen may not be permitted to go, but I suppose you will have more sense. The boats are loaded along the quay, and I have come to bear you to safety now."

He tried to lower his voice, so that he should be heard only by her, but it was not easy for him to do, his habit being to talk in a boisterous way, as one who calls to a crowd.

Raina looked at him in a way that he did not like, though he was not greatly perturbed. "Why," she asked, "do you offer this?"

"I shall be first in the fleet, and you are one who should be wife to the first of all."

"The fourth wife, I suppose?" she asked, and amusement tamed the contempt that she might have shown.

"That," he answered, "would be for me to resolve. But, in fact, there will be no other than you. The space for women will not be much, and they must be chosen with care."

"And where then do your wives go?"

"They must stay where they are, which will be to go, I suppose, where the King will lead. I prefer you."

"It is an honour I have not sought. You must make choice from the three you have."

Swashki's brow darkened, but not much. "This," he said, "is not a time for the wasting of words. You have heard my will.... If you thought to mate with the King, you would have found it the poorer choice, and Bira would have made sure that you would not have had a long joy, unless she have changed much from what she is said to have been before."

"But I have no purpose to wed, either with the King or with you."

Swashki saw that he must use plainer words.

"You are not asked. You are told. And you will do well to come with a good grace, for I have men below to enforce my will. Unless you would be whipped before you are wed, which you must suppose that I am equal to do."

Raina looked at him with eyes which, she must hope, did not show the fear which had shaken her heart, for she saw suddenly in what a trap she must be, if the King should be willing to let her go. And why should he trouble for that, having greater cares? She had been a poor goddess to this land, and might be better away when they should try escape in the night.

She looked past Swashki, to where her friends (if she could call them that, which was to be shortly proved) were still seated upon the floor. They were all looking her way, with some curiosity in the women's eyes, for Swashki had raised his voice in his last words, being impatient that she should cause a useless delay.

"We must talk," she said, "of this to the King."

"I will tell the King," he replied, "that you go with me. You will do well to assent, or to say nothing at all."

As he said this, he walked back to the King, and she was but little behind.

"I am taking the goddess," he said, "needing a good wife on the boat, such as I shall expect her to be."

Before Raina had chosen words to deny that, the King answered him in an easy way: "The goddess may do as she will, and she will say in her own time if it be her purpose to go with you. But that is not a matter for now, as I have work for which I need a good man, as I must judge you to be."

He went on to give the order for Swashki to attack those apes which had spread themselves in the southern houses toward the sea, of which he had spoken before he came.

Swashki listened, and resolved that he must make his position clear, as he felt equal to do.

"I must tell you this," he said, "and it will be best for all if you will take it in peace. I cannot do that, for the boats are nearly ready to sail, and I have planned to go in the next hour."

The King did not seem surprised or resentful of this. It seemed that there was nothing which he would not take in a quiet way, but Swashki saw the Queen's wrath, and knew, with a sudden surprise, that he must be wary of her, her hand being on the bone dagger within her belt.

Tela looked at him in the way she had, timid and yet composed, as one who watches a play which she does not share, though it may be sufficient to shake her heart. He thought nothing of her.

The King asked: "Do you tell me that you would leave your kinsmen and friends, while the strife is around our doors?"

"It is better," Swashki replied, "that some live than that all die.... You have chosen the way of the land, which I do not like.... And men can follow the one they will."

It cannot be known what the King would have answered to that, for Bira was quick to speak: "Do you tell us that your wives have chosen the land? Then they are wiser than I thought them to be."

Swashki flushed at that in an angry way, for her voice made her meaning clear, giving him a choice of scorns, whether he was to think that she believed him or not. He found, as had happened before when he was met with open contempt, that he had no words for reply.

Meanwhile the King said: "Well, you have picked your part. It is a time when men will show what they are at root, and I suppose that you think that my right as your King is done."

As he said this, he rose without haste from the floor, and the two women did the same.

Swashki felt that he had gained that for which he had come, and the Queen's rudeness irked him the less. He said to Raina: "You must come now. You can bring all that you can bear in two hands, but no more; and it must be gathered without delay."

"You have brought," the King asked, "a good guard?"

"I have brought enough."

The King repeated words he had used before Swashki came: "You are a bold and confident man." Swashki was deaf to the irony in the King's tone. He was pleased by praise which he felt to be no more than his due. He was glad that the King recognised facts in such a sensible way.

It seemed to Raina that she was abandoned by all. Should she decline to go, offering a resistance which could not prevail? Or should she seem to yield, that she might escape at a better time? And yet, what better time would there be likely to be? She looked round in doubt, and with an impulse to fly to the inner caves, where it would be hard for Swashki to make pursuit. She had been warned by Bira that they were not safe to attempt, even with the aid of a light. Without that, what could she hope but to stumble into their dreadful pits, or lose herself where she would not come forth alive?

But the King was speaking again: "Goddess, do you choose to go with this man of your own will?"

"No," she said, with a new hope. "I do not choose him at all."

"That may be as it will," Swashki said to the King. "I have chosen her." He turned to Raina to say: "If you will stretch no hands for your gear, you must come bare."

"The Goddess," the King said, as one who mentions that which is easy to see, "is in the Queen's care, from whose protection she cannot go, except of her own will."

Swashki was angered at that. He felt that he had had patience enough. "I have told you," he said, "that I have men waiting below. It will be best for all that she come in a quiet way."

Bira interposed again: "There is a stone which will crush any who climb that stair."

"But," Swashki replied, "being up, I am not under its fear."

He stood facing the King, with the Queen somewhat to the King's left, and Raina near at his other side. He did not scruple to front his King with a flint-head club threateningly in his hand. He was between them and the entrance to the cave, barring their way to the stone.

"It will be best," he said, "to give the goddess to me. For if you resist that, I shall call up my men, who may be much rougher than I."

"They will come," the Queen said, "to a sure death."

Swashki saw that he had taken the path of violence too far to retreat, whatever outrage it might now require to get him clear of that cave.

"I care not," he said, "whom it may be. If you move when I call them up, you are no better than dead."

The Queen laughed: "I always thought you a fool."

Swashki shouted for his men to come up. He did not venture to turn, watching the three who faced him without movement upon their side.

He heard voices and feet on the steps without, and then was startled by one voice that he heard alone. Tela called: "You will stand, if you are wise men."

There came an answering voice from the stair: "Priestess, we were called to come up."

"It was an order you should not have been quick to hear. You know the use of this stone?"

"Priestess, we know it well. But we were called, and we thought no ill."

"Listen," Tela replied, in the voice which the Old One had taught her to use at such times as these, "for I speak with a voice that is more than mine. You need have no fear of this stone from me. Your priestess does not shed blood. But I will tell you something that you should know. If you ascend these stairs, not having the Queen's word that she would have you to come, the order of your ascent is that in which you are doomed to die, and the latest death will not wait for a distant day."

Swashki knew now what the Queen had meant when she had called him a fool. He had failed to observe that Tela had drawn aside, and had gone to the head of the steps while he had been watching the other three. But she had not seemed to have any part in this, and her movements were always quiet, in an assured way that did not draw observation upon themselves.

Now he stood facing these three: one whom he must capture before he left, and two whom he felt would be a deadly menace, if his eyes should withdraw but for a moment from what they did, and there was a pause of silence, seeming to those four to be much more than it was, while he could not resolve what it would be best for him to do.

Should he slay his King, and the Queen also, for which the need might be no less? He did not think it beyond his power to do that, nor did any scruple invade his mind, and the goddess should then be easy to bear away.

But he had heard Tela's assurance to his men that the stone would not be tilted by her. Was not that enough to remove his most difficult dread?

He shouted to them to come up, which should surely be such a demonstration of force as would prevail without need for any shedding of blood. "Will you shiver for empty words? Let the priestess talk as she will, you will not die by a sooner hour."

He lacked the imagination which makes it easy to feel a dread of the unseen powers that surround the visible world. Tela, like Raina, was no more than another woman to him, unless she should be one to arouse his lust, which she did not do.

But the men muttered and feared. Had he been with them, example might have prevailed, or, had Tela met them with a more general curse, there might have been a slow advance, in which the bolder men would have come to the front, and which would have gained confidence in itself; but when they were told that they would be doomed in the order in which they ranged themselves on the steps, who would be self-sacrificial enough to place himself at the head? Who could expect that his comrades would be content for him to stand in the rearmost place?

Swashki called, but they did not come.

Then the full significance of what Tela had said entered his mind. A priestess did not shed blood. It was an ancient law, of which he had heard before, with a legend attached, to which he had paid no heed, for it would have put no food into him. All his days he had disregarded such things as were not helpful to his own comfort or pride. But he saw that if she would not shed blood she could be disregarded for herself, as well as one who would not put hand to the stone. Her power, which had been evil enough for him, had been to frighten his men.

132

He was not overclear in mind as to how this scruple of Tela would be helpful to him, but he knew the pleasure that it would be to kick that stone, and hear it leap to the ground, so that its menace would be no more. He shouted again to the men, still without turning his head: "If you dare not come up, stand away; or you may find a quick death where you are," which they were more willing to do.

He had his club in his hand, and the King's club was still hanging against his side. The King stood at ease, as one having no thought of a present strife, but Swashki did not doubt that the club would be in his hand before the four yards could be crossed by which they were now apart.

The Queen's hand was still on her dagger's hilt, and her face was dark with a fierce contempt, which was empty of fear. If he gave her a chance to strike, there was no doubt where that blade would be.

But her strength could be little to his. Could he not break her skull with one sweep of the club, and after that be quick enough for the King? Even thus, Raina might escape before he would be free for dealing with her.... But there was one thing he could do which must tend to simplify that which remained: he could settle that stone.

He moved backward, step by step, till he was standing at Tela's side. He would not take his eyes from the King, for a club can be quickly thrown. He did not expect the King to do that while he was watchful against the risk, for men were trained to dodge the coming of such a throw, and if it should pass a bent head, the King would be left unarmed; but if he should look aside it was likely that the next second would be his death. Without looking at what he did, he put a foot backward against the stone.

Tela saw it roll from its place, and crash down the stair. She saw something else, which it was not her business to say. The stone struck the floor of the cave, leaping into fragments thereat, and raising a cloud of dust in that vaulted place. Swashki's men, watching from round the outer entrance of the cave, were content that they had left that stair to itself.

Swashki heard the crash, and was content too. That stone had been on his mind. Now he felt prepared to deal with all in a more confident way. All men knew him (he thought) to be a man of great valour and strength. There were moments when his cunning was not equally clear to all: even when a doubt of himself might invade his pride. But now, with that backward kick, he had made sport of the defence of the cave on which the Queen so greatly relied, and by doing that he had also shown where the brains were.

Club in hand, and with a wary eye on the King, he strode up to Raina, with a gesture as of one who had been patient enough, and would wait no further delay.

She turned instinctively to the King, but did herself an ill turn in that, for she stood for a moment between the two, preventing that on which the King had resolved, and Swashki was quicker than she.

He had her arm in a hard grasp, and with the soft flesh in his hand he felt that she had come to his power, and the end was his.

"Will you yield in peace," he said, as she drew away with more strength than he had thought her to have, though it might be feeble to his, "or are you one who must be quietened with blows?"

She struck him for reply with all the strength of her free hand, calling as she did so for the King's aid, and in a moment there was turmoil within the cave.

Swashki swung her by the arm he held, flinging her against the wall so that her head struck, as he had meant it to do, and her senses went for that time. Even as he did this, he dodged the King's club, and struck back. The King swerved, so that his head took no more than a glancing blow, but it brought him down to his knee, where he would have been at the risk of another stroke, but, at the same moment, Bira's dagger thrust upward in Swashki's side.

He kicked her off, scarcely aware of his wound, or how deep it was, and saw his chance of escape as the King rose in a dazed way to renew the strife. He snatched Raina from the ground, throwing her to his shoulder lightly enough, as few men of his time would have been able to do, and hurled his club at the King, who could but ward it off on an arm which must take its bruise. The next moment he had pushed Tela roughly aside, and was descending the stair.

The stone steps were narrow and steeply cut, and could not be taken with speed by one who had not used them before, and was burdened besides; but he was halfway down when Bira followed him out, caring nothing for the hurt of a kicked leg, and knowing well what she meant to do.

"Oh, not that!" Tela exclaimed. "You will kill her too." But Bira took no notice of her. She stooped to a second stone, which had been concealed by the first, but was mounted on such a slant that it could be started with little toil when the support of the first was gone. Swashki might have seen this, if he had had eyes to spare, but it was a thing he was not likely to guess. He was near the foot of the stair when Bira let it leap free.

It struck him fairly across the back, sweeping him down the last steps, and seemed content with the place it had found, for where it had struck it remained, with Swashki spread-eagled beneath it upon the ground.

Raina, who had been half aware in a dizzy mind that she had been carried away, was cast clear of her captor's fall, and struck the ground with a jolt that did her no deadly hurt, but rather revived her to the life she had lost before.

She rose with some pain, and put a hand to her hair, to draw it reddened away.

She looked down at Swashki, crushed by a weight under which he could draw no breath, nor bring sound to his lips, though his eyes were alive in a face which it was not pleasant to see. Bira was down the steps now, with the King shortly behind. Tela stayed where she was, having no lust for the sight of the dying man, and being content to see that Raina had fallen clear of the stone.

The ten whom Swashki had brought stood round in a frightened group, seeing the King and Queen appear in the disorder of recent strife, and their master lie as he did.

Bira looked into the tortured eyes with the contempt she had shown before. She asked one who could not reply: "Did I not find the right word, when I called you fool?"

The King called to the ten to roll off the stone, which it was not easy to do, but when it was pulled away it did Swashki no good. The blood gushed from his mouth for a time, and then he lay still.

CHAPTER TWENTY-EIGHT

"You can take him out," the King said, "and throw him into the next ditch." It was not a time when any man could expect to be buried with care, and those of his race did not eat their own flesh, as the Ho-Tus were accustomed to do. And Swashki, at the best, would have been no better than fishes' food, having thrown his club at the King.

He looked at the stone, and said: "It should be lifted again if we had the use of a quieter time; but it was in my mind when I came here that you should remove to my own cave, where a troop could not enter without our will; though I suppose that this night will see them both vacant alike."

He asked of the Queen's hurts, which were not much, and then of Raina's, which she would not have him regard, and went off with no thought of his own wounds, having his mind filled with more urgent affairs.

The Queen (having bound her hurt, and Raina hers, with aid from Tela for both) was active to carry out that which the King's prudence had planned. She moved all that she valued most to the private cave of the King, which she had not entered before, and stored it with food, and with other things, even beyond what they could hope to bear away in the night; and even while they did this, and the slow hours passed in the summer sky, they were hastened by sounds of strife, dreadful and loud, and by frequent cries that would be distant or near, of those who came to the apes' teeth, and their comrades were weak to save.

It was late day before they saw more of the King, and when he came it could be seen that his strength was done for that time, for he had not spared himself on the front of a hopeless war.

The apes spread over the land, and the women and children fled, while the men held them back as much as they might, and here and there an ape died; but there was no evident gain in that, for it seemed that their number was such that it had no end.

136

The worst news that the King brought was that the apes had come again by the river path, and had forced that passage at last, so that there was no longer hope of escape by way of the Sacred Cave. "Unless," the King said, thinking a small chance to be better spoken than none, "they may retire during the night, leaving the way free."

"We can live," the Queen said, "at the worst, in your cave for a space of days, and though they overrun the whole land, yet they may become sated, and go while we hold our lives."

"That," the King replied, "is a bold thought, if there be nothing better to do. Is it garnished well?"

"Not so ill. But it shall be better done before night. I had not thought it a large chance that we should be cornered here."

"It is more than chance. It is a most likely thing.... But here Plini comes, whom I had thought to be at the boats."

The King had given Plini control of the boats and quays, and he had ordered all in a way that Swashki would have thought poor. He would not allow that men should leave their women behind, nor any children that the sickness had spared, neither would he have the boats loaded with such as would not have kept them afloat through the next storm, nor be of; the best avail if they should come to a good landing at last. He ordered that with each man his whole household should be embarked, neither more nor less, and that, if there were more who wished to escape by sea than the boats would bear (as it was plain that there must be as the day waned, and the apes prevailed), the choice should be made by lot. And as each boat was prepared, and took on as much folk as it could safely contain, it was rowed out some distance to sea, and anchored there to await the rest of the fleet.

So the loading of boats had gone on through the day, while such men as were of good courage and strength fought on all sides to hold the apes further away than they were striving to come, to give space and time for such things as it was still needful to do.

Now Plini said: "I have the last boats at the quay, and of these I have a good one emptied apart for yourself and yours. So I came to say; for it seems that there can be no safety on and by another dawn."

The King said: "You have done well. But as to this empty boat, the Queen may go if she will. And the priestess is one who should not be left. She should go with those who can save themselves, for they will be the tribe in the coming years, and a priestess they ought to have. But they must find a new King for themselves, for I do not think it my part to seek safety upon the sea, leaving half the nation to die."

The Queen said: "I shall stay here." She did not praise herself for that choice. She added: "I call it the better place, for I have no love for the sea, which I never sailed."

Tela looked at them in a quiet way, and would have said nothing at all, had she not been asked for a second time. Then she said no more than: "It is with the Queen I shall stay." She would have liked to add: "I am no priestess at all. It is no more than one of the lies that are dead, as I suppose, with the loss of the Sacred Cave." But what use was there in that?

She was reminded of one of the tablet writings which had troubled her thoughts a few days before. It had said: "*No race can outlast its gods*," as though warning her of a great duty she had, and making even that which was base and false in itself, in the rituals to which she was heiress beyond her will, an obligation to keep alive; as though even a lying faith were of the nature of heart or lungs, which, however diseased or defective they may become, are yet too vital to be cut out and the body live.

Was it no more than proof of the morbidity of the race that Swashki spoke to her without respect, and even Plini (she thought) regarded her less as one Sacred and Highly Apart than as a girl to be saved by the care of her natural lords?

She felt that such matters were too great for her to resolve, though she was long used to the companionship of lonely and wandering thoughts. But did it matter now? For it was plain that they had either come to the end of all, or else to a new time, which might be found by those who went the way of water and wind. But she had no liking to go, it being too great a change from what her life had been from its birth till the last days, and that reluctance turned to resolve when she saw that her parents stayed. She did not say this in words of which the meaning would have been plain, for the fiction that she was not born in a natural way was not yet to be cast aside.

Plini seemed less willing to accept Tela's resolve than those he had heard before, but he saw much with his single eye, and he knew that she spoke that which she would not change.

Raina observed that she was not asked what she would choose, though she supposed that it would not have been denied had she said that she wished to go. She was over thought; and she had the feeling again that she was friendless in a place to which she did not belong, which may have been less than fair to those who did not let Swashki bear her away.

The King said: "It is to you I entrust the fleet; and when I do that, I know that I give it to the charge of a good man. It may be, if we survive the war that the apes have made (or which we rather began ourselves, for which I take the most blame) we shall meet again on a far day; or our children will hear of where we have wandered apart. But that may be long away, if it ever come.... You should go now, and draw clear of a leeward shore while the light prevails."

"But," Plini replied, "by your leave, I am not going that way. I am a man of the land. I arrayed the fleet; but I did that as being the charge which you gave me to do. But (by your leave again) as to myself, I will stay here."

The King looked at him in some doubt. It seemed that, if that was what he had meant, he might have said it before. But there was nothing in Plini's eye to raise a doubt that it was what he meant now, and that he would be more cheerful to stay than to take his leave.

"If I agree to that," the King asked, "who will control the fleet in your place?"

"As to that," Plini replied, "it has leaders enough." (He named some of these.) "And it is not sure that they would have taken orders from me. As I think, it will break apart; which may be the best way. It will scatter to different fates; and some will die, and some live."

"Well," the King said to that, "so it may be. You will have message sent that they can put off. But, for myself, I must have some rest, for the time has come when I have no strength to do more."

CHAPTER TWENTY-NINE

THE King slept (having said that he must be waked again when the darkness came), which may have been well both for him and his, but was less so for those who clamoured, as evening approached, to be let into the cave. He might have opened to those whom the apes pursued till the cave were filled with more than it would have been easy to feed, but Bira was a woman of different ways. "We will not begin that," she said, "which it would not be easy to stop."

It seemed, as the hours passed, that the apes had spread over the whole land, and when Plini resolved to observe with his own eye whether the river path were held, or in what force, he found that he had started upon a very perilous way. The Queen let him in, when he came back to report, and she let in one other, for Huni came in the dusk, being more dead than alive, and able to say that he had brought no news that would not keep till the King waked.

"It is near time," the Queen said, "that we wake him now."

"He was to be roused," Plini said, "as I suppose, that he might lead those who still live to the way of the sacred cave. But you need not wake him for that. The apes swarm on that side, and, as you can judge by the cries without, they are round us on every path. If we should leave here there is no way we could go but we might be their meat in the next hour."

He spoke with evident truth, and as to the approach to the Sacred cave, the fact was that the apes had come down again by the Cliff of Thorns, with a clear plan that they would overrun the whole land on that side, from their own heights to the sea, with the design that there should be no way left open for men to escape, either to north or south.

Now they herded them from both ends, between cliffs and sea, leaving no better hope but to do the apes the most damage they could as themselves died. Their cries did not cease, though they quietened somewhat as darkness closed.

The King slept, if he can be called a king whose nation has left his rule, or is no better than dead; and Bira had the lamps lit, in contempt of the apes without, who might see the gleam, if they would, through the chinks of the closing stone, for it was so shaped that to batter it from without would but fix it the more.

After a time, Bwene waked of himself, and his eyes fell on Huni, who lay against the wall in an exhaustion that sleep could not conceal.

"Why," he said, "is he here? You should have called me without delay. Is the word good?"

"He said it would be no worse if it kept," Bira replied, "and he was so spent that I let him lie."

"Well so we all are. But I should say, by his looks, that he did not come through the apes by an easy road. He must wake now, and his tale be told."

Bira, whose courage was not of the kind to deceive itself, thought that it could be of little present moment to them though the Ho-Tu king should pay them to cross his land, they being penned as they were, and those of their nation who had not fled by the sea being now skulking or slain; but it was no time to debate that.

She spoke to Plini, who used his foot mildly enough, and Huni came awake with a start of fear.

"I can see," the King said, "that you have come a difficult way, but I suppose, if nought else, that you have the use of your jaw, and, in a word, have you done that for which you were sent?"

"I have done nothing," Huni replied. "I have been done to."

"You have left your companions," the King supposed, "you having broken down on the way?"

"I have left them," Huni agreed, "but not so that you will see them again. They are today's meat for the Ho-Tus."

"You had better tell us this tale," the King said, "from the right end. It is plain to see that its finish is not one that we need be hurried to hear."

Huni was content to do that. It was a tale that was lurid enough, without adding of colour by him, but the Ho-Tus did not dwindle in number or bulk, nor in the way they licked their chops for a coming meal, as he told it now.

When he got to the place where they were cooped up by the wives of the chief (whom he would call king), he went on:

"So we were hurried by these women, who are as busy and black as ants, but taking life in a less serious way, to the rear of the king's house, the dogs growling and smelling around our legs. We were put into a wooden shed, and given food, which was good. The women were joking about us, with gestures which were easy to understand, though their speech is unlike to ours.

"They made signs, which were plain enough, for they did not scruple in what they did, that we must eat, or we should be slaughtered without delay. But we were glad enough to do that, being hungered and very tired by the pace at which we had run through all the heat of the day."

"You say you had run many hours?" the King asked. He looked at Huni, thinking he could never have done so much, and pondering how much he could take for true.

Huni was a wise man, and he knew the King. The question was quietly put, but it warned him that he who says less may be believed more.

"I cannot tell how far I had run or how long, for I was dazed with exhaustion, and sick with fear, and when the black shadow was overhead, I spurted forward again;"

Huni, who was sitting on the ground as he told his tale, looked over his shoulder as he said this, and up to the roof of the cave, as though the black giant he feared had been of a height of twenty feet, if not more.

"Well," the King allowed, "I can see that terror has used your limbs more than they would have moved for any order of mine. Tell me why you are not now being stewed for the soup which is about all that they would have swallowed from you."

Huni looked sulky at that. He had not wished to be a roast on the board of the Ho-Tu chief, but the contempt with which the King regarded his legs was an annoyance of a different kind.

"We were left there," he went on, "for a time, the women going away, though we could hear them laughing afar, and the dogs were left round the door, which was barred on the outside in a solid style, for it is a land in which wood is no more worth than is the sand on our own shore.... We talked of how we could make escape, but we were too weary to plan or act, and so we agreed that we must rest, and begin to plan on the next day.

"But after that the Ho-Tu king came to see us again. There were then other women around his heels, for we were, as I suppose, a show which he did not mean them to miss.

"I think we were all asleep when he came, which may show how wearied we were, but we were soon roused, and he must have us out, the roof being too low for his head, though the women ran in and out of the door with ease.

142

"When he had looked at us again, he had the others put back into the shed, but he ordered that I should be taken another way, and put into a place apart, being given more food than before, and with the signs that I must eat or die being made again. So I began to eat while they looked on, which I thought it safest to do, though it was with less heart than before."

The King said: "You were always a prudent man. But will you come to how you escaped? Or did they change their minds, and let you run free, as not being worth the cost, when they saw how much food you could put away?"

Huni was offended again. He thought the King made a jest of what had been done to him, and he had heard laughter enough from Ho-Tu lips to content him for many days. He would have refused to say more to another man, or have answered in a way to make feeling plain, but he knew that he must take what the King gave, and he went on to tell of how he had escaped in the night.

"I was in a separate shed, it may have been sixty or eighty yards from the one I had left, but I cannot say surely how far, for the place was so thick with trees, among which we twisted about. There were staples in the wall, and chains hanging therefrom, of some metal I do not know, and the women who brought me, of whom there may have been six, and as many dogs (which I feared more), looked at these chains, and I thought that they were about to fasten me to the wall; but when they had handled them for a time, they left them be.

"I suppose they saw that they were meant to contain such as are much larger than I."

"Perhaps they were," the King said. "But will you tell us, in fewer words, how you come to be here now?"

"I will tell it in the least words that I can. I climbed to the roof, and I dropped a block on the dog's head, and I came away.

"Was there only one dog?"

"Did you not order that I should make it a short tale? There was but one dog that was left during the night at the outside of my shed. Had I been able to get the chains loose from the wall...."

"Never mind the chains," the King interposed. "Did you do nothing to set your companions free?"

"To rouse the dogs that were round their door? And to be torn apart, which would have been no comfort to them? I had enough trouble upon my hands to find my way here."

"Well," the King allowed, being a just man, "I do not say you could have done more. Did you find the boat where it was left? Were you unseen by the apes when you rowed it back?"

"The boat was there, but I let it remain, thinking that if my companions should have escaped, they might come to it at greater need, and the river was not more than I was able to swim."

"That," the King said, "was well done.... You have done," he pronounced, in a different tone from that which he had been using before, "as much as a man might, and more than many would have contrived to bring to a good end.... And you have made it plain that we can look neither for mercy nor aid from these savages of the woods, who are yet, as it must appear, of higher race than ourselves, for they thrive, while we are hustled and die."

"Yet," Huni objected to that, for he had endured too much to be eager to hear them praised, "they had not so much wit but that I have come free of their hands; by which it may be said that they are less than ourselves."

"If you are so good at getting free from a trap's jaws," the King answered to that, "you can try it a second time; for you have done no more, as it seems, than to wander from snare to snare. But as to whether we be the better men, or else the apes, or the Ho-Tus, it is that which the end will prove; for which, as I suppose, the gods watch the way the scale tilts, as men may look at a show. And there may be times when they interpose, as is held by some, though it is less easy to think, for it is sure that they do not do that in a visible way.

"But if they watch now, I suppose they may call the Ho-Tus, or even the apes, of the better breed."

CHAPTER THIRTY

BWENE could think of gods, and of the values of apes and men, even while his people were slain, and their minds, as we may be sure, were full enough of their own ills; and we may say that that was because he was in a safe cave, with a strong stone at its door. But that is less than the truth, for it is the part of a good king ever to ponder and watch, so that it is a habit the years will fix; and it is likely that his thoughts would have walked in the same way had he known that he would not live to the next dawn, unless there had been others for whom he must still contrive; for it is by service only that kings endure.

Having heard Huni's tale, and being rested by the sleep he had had, Bwene turned his mind to enquire as to the provision within the cave, concerning which he found that Bira had done well enough; though he would have said that she had given too much of her time to the bearing of trifles that women love, even such as she, from her own cave, when she had seen that it must be left for the apes to plunder, or for those of her own kind (it might be) to turn over that which had been precious to her, having been gathered through many years to her private hoard.

Strung dozens of salted fish had been borne into the cave, with store of the dry biscuits or cakes which was made from the buckwheat flour which was the growth of a shallow soil, and which were so made that they would last till the next harvest should be ready to reap.

It was dry, tasteless food, and may have told why the nation had sickened since it had settled upon that land, but it was what they were customed to have, and had the virtue that it would not spoil for a far day.

The cave was not as spacious as were those of the Queen, having been the King's choice only because it could be made secure from within, but it was alike in that it was an approach to others that ran far back to a distance no man could guess. The King had not gone far to explore that which was dark and he did not need, but now there must be some moving inward of those who would not sleep on the same floor, and exploration for water, which the caves would not be seldom to yield, having within their depths many pools which were cold and pure.

"We can endure here," the King said, "for a long space, if we must. And I would that we had taken in more of our folk from the peril which lies without."

The Queen said nothing to that, thinking that she had contrived in a better way. There was herself, and Tela whom she was glad to have, and Raina whom she could have spared with no grief, and for whom she might still have designed a quick end, had she foreseen that which was soon to be; and there were three men alike, of whom Plini and Huni would, as she saw, be useful to wait on the women and on the King, and both (as she thought) be such as it would be little trouble to rule.

She thought that this six was enough to be so cooped, for she held that those of a royal rank should not mix with commoner men, and she supposed that the apes would retire, at most, in a few days, when they had wasted the land. Nor did she doubt that there would be then enough of men left, and of women also (of whom there had been too many before) whom the apes would not have been active enough to slay, and who could follow the King to wherever he should resolve that it would be prudent to go.

But, for the time, there could be no difference on this point between her and the King, for the apes were gathered closely around the mouth of the cave, as though they knew that something of value were closed therein.

It was likely that this was due to the lights that the Queen had set, which were more than the cave had held till that day, for she had brought her own lamps, with good measures of oil, and fixed them about the sides of the cave, and of some inner chambers that she would have brought into use. The stone did not fit so closely that no rays of light would shine out, of which the most would be made by a night that was too misty for stars to show. Men who had loved the light till that day were now better content to crouch in the darkest corner that they could find, hoping that they would be overlooked by the apes, and so this light, being alone, had become a beacon for the collecting of foes.

"It matters nought," the King said, "though they be in hundreds without, for there is no force that could move that stone, unless it be scraped in powder away, and will the apes try to do that? Let them fret without as they will."

Plini examined the stone. He found a place near the ground where, if he gave it an upward thrust, his spear would go through. He waited till he could hear a sound of apes fumbling without, and then gave it a strong thrust. It sank through something soft, and struck bone. It was wrenched about, so that he was glad to get it back whole. There was a sound without, between a sob and a snarl, and then a loud chattering of the queer sounds that the apes would make when they were excited or wroth.

"It is likely," he said, "that he I reached will have killed one man, if not more, since the dawn came; but I have given him something other of which to think, so that he will make no boast about that. I would I could give such a thrust to every ape in the land."

He listened long for another chance; but it seemed, after that, that they kept further away.

Chapter Thirty-One

"I WOULD be told," the King asked of Tela, "how you could lead men in the dark by that secret way, so that they came out at last in the higher land?"

"It is less easy," Tela replied, "to say than to do. But you must know, in the first place, that I am not lost in the dark, as is a man whose whole comfort is in the light of the sun, or when a fish-fat candle is near. I can see much better than they, but the answer is not wholly in that; for though I can see in a little light, I must have some, and, in the utmost depth of the caves, the darkness has no leaven of light at all.

"It is, in part, that I can feel things that I do not see, while they are yet some distance away, so that, be it the most absolute dark, I cannot stumble into a pit, nor bruise myself on a wall's side.

"I could not guard myself by such means so that I might not be lost in the endless caves that wander far under the land, but that the Old One traced them for many miles, and has named them with markings that can be felt.

"But the upward part of the way of which you ask is found by memory of crossings and turns, and, when the walls fail, by a careful counting of steps, and by four small pools that lead in a curving way to where there must be a turn taken, sudden and sharp, or else there would be a fall to what depth I have little guess, but a stone falls so far that there will be nothing to hear."

"Well," the King said, "I would not be the one to lead the way on that track, but I suppose it is nothing to you."

"It is much to me; though I do not mean that it is a risk that I need to fear. And I should say that it gave the Old One much joy to trace in the long darkness that a priestess must learn to endure (but I suppose that to be over now), as did her carving upon the rocks, which it may be, from this day, that no man will ever see."

"Do you suppose," the King asked, this being the question that filled his mind, "that there may be another way of escape, of a like kind, through the caves that are behind this?"

"How can I say? But I do not think it a likely thing, for the floor of all the caves is level, except for that single ascent, and these (as far as I have yet seen) are alike; and we know that the higher land is very far up. But I would search with a good will."

"You must take no peril for that, which would be a higher price than I am willing to pay."

"There is no peril if two go, for the risk is but of a slip, and, it may be, a laming hurt where you could not lightly be found."

"Well, you can take Plini along."

"I would take Huni rather than him."

"Then you have a poor choice. Huni is a good man with his tongue, and of subtle mind, but he is no better than that."

Tela did not dispute this. She may have agreed; but she had a woman's reason that none should say that the choice of Plini had been hers.

It came to the same end, as she may have guessed that it would, for Huni said that he had a sore leg, which he had hurt when he had leapt from the roof of the hut where he had been confined by the Ho-Tus, which (he said) was getting worse, rather than well; and whether it were true, or the pretence of one who did not wish to wander into the caves, was not easy to know.

But Plini went with a ready will, though he must trim his torches with care, not being one for whom the darkness was any friend, and in the next two days they had wandered far, marking every turning they passed, so that they had no fear that they could not return, though it seemed that the caves must spread for ever beneath the land.

On the second day, they came back after being absent for many hours.

Tela said: "We have found a way to the Queen's cave. It is a long way, for it is needful to go far before you can turn back as you would, but when the turn is made, you can go straightly enough."

"Did you enter my cave?" the Queen asked. She looked troubled, or else displeased, as Tela had not thought that she would have reason to be.

"We could not do that. It was full of apes. We watched them for a time, from such darkness that they could not guess we were there."

The Queen did not seem to mind that. It was clear that her annoyance (if such it were) was not caused by any fear that others might make free with her cave.

Plini added: "The apes seemed afraid, as though they were glad to hide, rather than with the look of those who take what we have been forced to leave. Perhaps they had quarrelled among themselves."

"We will look out at dawn tomorrow," the King said, "when it is not likely that there will be many about. They must be tired of watching a stone that is never moved."

It was clear that it would be a great risk to move back the stone without knowing how many apes might be await to rush in, but, till they did that, they could know nothing of the strength that confined them there, or what was happening without, and it seemed time for it to be done.

"Yet," the King said, "I have no hope of a good sight, for were they gone, and my people alive, there would have been sound of human voices without before now, and this is a poor tale, of apes that sit in the Queen's cave, whether they be merry or sad."

"Well," Plini said, "so it was. We can but tell what we saw, whether it were evil or good; but I say again that they looked as sick as an ape can be."

"Perhaps," the Queen said, "that was why they were there." Which seemed to be as good a guess as they were likely to make. They must wait to see what the dawn would show.

CHAPTER THIRTY-TWO

THE King, whose use it was, tilted the great stone back in its groove, and stood ready to heave it again into its place, if there should be need to do it with haste. The greatest risk (which may not have been much) was that there might have been apes standing ready without, to thrust in some impediment, such as a heavy beam, which would have made it vain to attempt to return the stone. And next to that, that there might have been those who stood ready to shoot missiles within the cave. The apes had seen that there were men who were sheltered within, and the lights must have been visible every night. They had clustered closely around, until one of them had been hurt by the upthrusting of Plini's spear. It was hard to guess what patience or persistence they would be likely to show, but it was clear that they had not gone, for had they not been thickly gathered in the Queen's cave?

The King moved the stone, and Plini stood at hand with a back-drawn spear. The women waited aside, as the King required, and Huni had the excuse of his leg (of which he complained more as the days passed) that he should not rise.

"Well," Plini said, "I may stretch my neck to look out, but I could not see less had I let it stay as it was. I see nothing at all."

He had put forward a cautious head, lest there should be some who were lurking close, though they might not be in front of the cave. But there was nothing there, except a dead man on the ground, and his death was not new.

The King left his hold on the stone, and stood at his side. They went out a few yards, looking about, and still seeing a silent land.

"It seems," the King said, "if the apes have gone, that it was not till they had slain all. There is little comfort in that."

"It is less than a day that they had not gone, for they sat in the Queen's cave."

"Well, if you say that, we will not go far. We will leave it another day."

So the King said, but step followed step, till they had come further out than it may have been prudence to do, though the ground was open and vacant on either side of the cave.

"Unless," he went on, "they come out either from the Queen's cave, or the Cave of Words" (which was near, but somewhat beyond that), "I see not how they can be a threat to us as we stand here, and even then we should have time to get back, and to swing the stone."

But having walked as near to those caves as it was not rashness to do, and seeing no movement of any life, they went back, and, the women having come out by that time, they all stood round the cave, being glad of the light and the better air; except that Tela stood somewhat back, the sunlight vexing her more than she would have been willing to tell, for she felt it to be a defect, now that she was companioned by those who saw in another way.

Even Plini's one eye could face the sun better than her two, and could see more on a summer day.

She said: "We might go again to the Queen's Cave, and see from within whether the apes are still there," to which Plini agreed.

"If they be as sick as I thought they were, we might make some slaughter among them," he said. "We might go by night, and find them asleep."

He said this to the King, being a man of quiet speech, but of a persistence which was not easy to turn. He thought of the human dead, and he had become to the race of apes an implacable and untiring foe.

Having come back to the mouth of the cave, the King talked for a time to the Queen there, for he was reluctant to go in, and to close the stone.

"Perhaps," he said, "we have looked too early abroad. There may be more life in the next hour."

He felt that there must be things to be learnt that he ought to know. He walked out a short distance again, taking the opposite way from that they had gone before, and Plini came again at his side. The women, being more timid, or of a wiser prudence than he, stood about at the cave mouth. They let their eyes wander abroad, but their feet were still.

Gazing thus, it was Raina who saw first what the danger was. "Look!" she cried, "they are not apes. What are they?" And then she thought what they were. "They must be the Ho-Tus."

They may not have been as large as Huni had told, but they were huge men, and of a blue-black skin that shone in the sun, for their arms were bare, as were their legs under the knee. There were no more than eight, but they looked enough, being the size they were, and having great broad-bladed spears in their hands, by which that which Plini bore would have seemed no more than a bodkin for sewing clothes.

They had not seen the little group that was now gazing at them, for their way was toward the entrance of the Queen's Cave, and they were not looking aside. They hurried on, as those will who have sport in view.

Bira looked toward the King and Plini, who had their backs alike to the Ho-Tus and to those who would warn them if they could do it in a safe way. They were walking on, so that each moment it would be more hard to return.

"If we call," she said, in a great doubt, "the Ho-Tus will hear."

She spoke to Raina, for Tela had turned into the cave the moment before, and she had not yet seen what the danger was.

If a call should arouse at once the King and the Ho-Tus, it was hard to guess who would be first at the cave mouth, for who could tell at what pace those giant forms might be able to get over the ground?

"There is but one way," Raina said, "I must let them know." She ran after the King.

Bira turned back into the cave. There was no use in being seen at its mouth, and Raina would run no faster because she were watched by her. The King knew the way back. She said to Huni: "You know how this stone is worked. You must get on your legs, and stand ready to heave it in."

Huni groaned, saying he could not rise for the pain he had. It seemed that the hurt to his leg was more than a fancied ill. But Bira looked at him, and he made effort to rise....

It was the morning before that the three chiefs of the Ho-Tus had come to the land. They came for sport, not for war. They speared apes. The apes could run, if they would, when they would be speared through the back; or they could stand and leap at a foe that they would not reach, and be speared in front, that being all the choice that they had when the Ho-Tus came.

The Ho-Tus had hunted the land through the day, till the only apes that remained were those who had been quickest to flee, and the roar of the laughter of those who chased them and overtook would have been heard in the King's cave, but that it was one to which noise would not come freely from far when its stone was closed.

Now there was a party which had heard that apes still lurked in the Queen's cave, and they were eager to catch them there, after having supposed that their sport was done. Their comrades were busy tying dead apes by the legs in bundles of two or three, that they might bear them away. It was such a hunt as they seldom had, even in the rich lands of the south, and there would be much meat for the coming days in the homes of the Ho-Tus.

Raina ran lightly and fast, while the King and Plini walked in the slow manner of those who have no object to reach. When she was near behind, she called in a low voice, at which they turned, and what they saw was simple to understand.

"We could not call," she said, "lest they heard."

"It is what you should not have done, to come thus. Is the cave closed?"

The King thought it might be safer to hide than to run back in full view of the Ho-Tus, who, at any moment, might look their way. And that would be surely so if the Queen had thought it prudent to close the cave, and they would run back to an entrance they could not win.

"No," she said, the idea coming strangely to her, "they would not do that."

The King was less sure. He knew Bira was not a coward, but he knew also that, if her reason urged, there was little that she would scruple to do. He saw also that it might have been the best way, if it could have been understood, for it might be safer to hide than to go back now, while they must be seen by the first of the Ho-Tus who should turn his head.

"But so they might," he said, "and I should not say it was wrong."

He was, indeed, more inclined to take cover than to return. But if the cave were being kept open for them.... "Well," he said, "it should soon be done." It was so resolved in less time than it takes to tell.

The King ran at Raina's side, thinking that she should not be left who had come for him; but, in fact, her speed was equal to his. Plini ran at the same pace, though he could have outdistanced both, being the younger and slimmer man.

The Ho-Tus were now a group round the entrance to the Queen's cave. They did not go too close at the first, lest the apes, being cornered there, should come out with a rush. They did not wish to be hurt themselves by any rashness of risk, for it was hunting to them, not war. They looked in the lower cave, and saw that no apes were there, whereat most of them had gone in, when it was a mere chance that one at the back should look round, and see three who ran, not away, but as though they were eager to join the sport.

He put a hand on a neighbour's arm. "Now what," he asked, in the Ho-Tu tongue, "may that be?"

He did not see the cave entrance to which they ran, nor did he think there was any haste to meet those who seemed so hasty to come to him, but his companion had better eyes, or it may be that he used them more.

He shouted "Hoo!"—which was the Ho-Tu cry of the chase, with which they would start their dogs—and ran swiftly toward the three, with a great spear lifted to throw.

By this time, the three were much nearer than he to the place where they would be, and they would have made it with ease had their legs been of the length of his. As it was, they were first there, and Bira, who had watched well, though she had not allowed herself to be seen, had not given Huni the word that would have heaved the stone into place, making their fates sure, though it may have been near her lips.

It was an entrance that only one could pass at a time, and the seconds were few. The Ho-Tu who was first saw that he could not reach before they would go to earth, and he brandished his spear to throw.

The King pushed Raina in first. He would have been last, thinking that to be the place which a king should keep for himself, but Plini drew back, lifting the vain defence of his own spear against the rush of the blue-black giant. The King saw that to pause would be fatal to both. He followed Raina into the cave. The Ho-Tu flung a spear that was straightly aimed, but fell short, striking the ground between Plini's feet.

Had he delayed to throw but one second more, Plini would have been a dead man. As it was, the next spear, which came from his comrade behind, struck a closing stone, and Plini, who could be cool at an urgent pass, was inside, with the weight of a Ho-Tu spear in his hands, which he had caught up as it quivered against the ground.

CHAPTER THIRTY-THREE

THERE were sounds of Ho-Tu laughter without, and a voice of wrath, being his who had lost his spear. It seemed by the sounds that all the Ho-Tus must have left the apes, for the lure of a different hunt. So it was. They had killed many apes in the last day, and here was a chance of mixing the bag, which they would not miss. The stone shook to a force such as it had not been meant to feel, but those who were within were not greatly afraid.

They did not think that the Ho-Tus could force a way in, and, at a great need, they could retreat to the inner caves, with Tela for guide, where it was sure that the hunters would not pursue as far as they would be willing to fly.

The King said to Raina: "It was bravely done, which I will not forget." The thought that she would make a good wife would not leave his mind in these days, and the desire for that was like a thirst that he could not still, though he did not think that Bira would take it as a first wife who does not bear should be willing to do. He had a different doubt of what Raina might think, but with some hope that she might be brought to accord.

Bira said: "It was rashly tried, and came nearly to cost your life. You should have hid till they went away."

The King could not say that she was wrong about that. He thought silence best.

Plini looked at a spear that was eight feet long, of which three feet were the blade of a metal, polished and keen, that he did not know. It was a weight that he could lift, but not fling. He respected strength. He was glad that they had hunted the apes. He knew now why those had looked sick whom he had seen in the Queen's cave. They had been hiding, and sick with fear such as they had caused before to those of his own kind. He said: "They are men of might. How can we hope to endure in a world of such sorts as they?"

Yet he did not despond, having a heart that was both stubborn and strong, and which was alive with his own dreams. For what though it was held that a priestess can never wed? Had she not talked at times, when they had been alone in the caves, in a woman's way? He did not doubt that she w as better than he, nor that she was one to whom he would not have lifted a thought in a settled time. But could she be priestess more to a nation that was scattered or slain? And is not a man with one eye good enough, when those with two are not easy to find? He had the hope of a good end, though, as yet, it might be doubtful and far....

After a time, the voices of the Ho-Tus ceased, and it seemed that they had gone off. But for how far, or how long? It was agreed with ease that the stone should not be withdrawn again for that day.

Plini said: "If we could see how the apes fare in the Queen's Cave, we might learn something by that."

Tela said she would be his guide, if he would; for what else was there that they could do? The King said he would make a third; for he would see for himself what this way might be from his cave to that of the Queen, which had been found when its chances of any use might be near to none. Plini would have been more content had there been one less, but it was not a thing to be spoken aloud. Bira and Raina, being alike only in that, had no love for the dark ways that burrow under the earth. They made no motion to go. Huni lay on the ground, moaning his leg. The Queen looked at him, and thought that it might be an ill thing if a time should come when they must journey over the ground, or below, and be hindered by one with a damaged leg. She said: "I will see what the hurt may be."

When she had seen, she said: "When you cut it thus, as you came from the roof of the shed, why did you not cleanse it with better care? I have seen men die from such hurts."

Huni said: "Was there time for that? There was a dog that was not dead."

The Queen said: "Well, it is your leg. It gives me no pain." But she did what she could to dress it, and Raina helped her in that. This was after the party had split, and three had gone into the blackness behind the cave.

It was for two hours that the King was led in the dark through ways that he did not like. There were places where he must go with a bent head, the roof being so low. There were others which were foul with damp, or where he must wade through a black flood, with a rough surface beneath, so that there was no knowing to what depth he might go at the next step. There were places of sudden drops, or of deep pools, where Tela would call to him to follow closely, or step with care, as he was certain to do.

157

"Why," he thought, "should men go to the grave, while they still live?" And with the thought a fear came that Tela might make mistake, as all men will, sooner or late, and they might be lost, and wander further under the ground, ever further away from the cheerful light to which they would seek return till their strength would go. His heart beat at that fear in a panic way, such as it had not done when he raced for life with the Ho-Tus; but Tela's voice came to him again, and it was quiet and serene, as of one who was at home in a place she knew.

And so, when he had lost any sense of where he might be, or much hope that he would see sunlight again, there was a point of light, distant and dim, and Tela cautioned that he should cease speech, and step in a noiseless way, for the Queen s cave was not far.

But they found that the need for silence was less for the noise that met them as they approached. There was nothing that they could see, for this way to the cave ended in a slit in its high wall, and the point of light which guided them there came from one of those openings in its outer side that was at the same height.

They came at last to where they could look down, as men look into a pit of bears, and as they did this the noise lessened and stilled, for the most of the apes were already dead.

They saw that the Ho-Tus had come back to the sport for which they had set out at the first, and were now making an end. Some were now bundling the dead, and two were busy tying up a brace of apes that they had taken alive.

Plini felt that he could love them for what they did, though he knew that they would have been willing to treat those who looked down in the same way; but they had no guess that they were overseen, nor care for what any men might think concerning themselves, either bad or good. They slung the dead apes over their backs, and went laughing away.

"The apes," the King said, as they went back, "may have gone for this time, and may be slow to come back again. And the Ho-Tus may stay in their own land, thinking that the hunting would be less good on another day, but I would take the chance of the waste ways of the earth rather than stay here, being the six that we now are, and with such neighbours about our doors."

He spoke, as he had not done before now, of the salt marshes which lay to the north and were no more than the way to a barren desolate land, but, if they should go far enough, who could say to what they might not come? And there may be safety in barren lands, for those who are weak and few.

Tela, who had been silent for a long time before this, asked, as one who does not speak in an idle way: "Would you go now by the way of the Sacred Cave, if I could guide you to that?"

"Yes," he said, after a silence of thought, "so I would. But I would not go if it must be by the river path, lest the apes watch, whether for straggling of men, or that they may still fear the Ho-Tus, and we be all ended at once."

"But," she said, "there will be no need to do that, for I have learned a new thing. As we came away, and were but two turns from where the light can be seen, I looked, as it chanced, on an opening we leave aside, and the torch you bore shone on its wall, and there was a carving thereon that the Old One made, being one she had taught me well."

"You mean," he asked, "that by that sign you can lead us out to the higher land, or (if we should so require) to the Sacred Cave?"

"Yes," she replied. "Those are things which it would be simple to do. But it is strange that the Old One should have come so near to the Queen's cave and yet not have known that it was not more than two turnings away."

"It were hard," the King said, "to tell what the Old One knew, so I will spare the words of a vain guess.... But you have changed doubt to resolve. We will rest well this night, and tomorrow until the evening is near, and after that you shall decide how much of the things you own you are willing to bear, for I hope to be far across the high land of the apes before the moon will have begun to lighten the sky."

When they got back, the Queen heard what Tela had found, and the King resolved, at which she showed little surprise, and no pleasure at all. But when the King talked of what they were to take as being portioned for six, she asked: "Do you call us that? There are but five who will go."

Then she told of the state of Huni's leg, "which," she said, "is not such that he could walk well in a week's time, even should it be speedy to mend: and, as I think, it will not, so that he is more likely to die. You should not hinder for him."

The King considered this, and though there was that in her tone which he did not like, there was reason which he could not deny. At the extreme to which those who remained alive had been driven now, it was a king's part to care for the hale, rather than to let them delay for the spent and lame, such as could be of no further avail....

And for Huni there was little that could be said. He could not strike as a man, for his strength was spent: he was not a woman, so that he could not bear: and as to wisdom, the King did not doubt that he could himself supply that which occasions require. As a king, in which way he must still think of himself, though it might be of no more than a feeble few, it was his plain duty to put Huni aside, and think of those by whom the tribe might be rooted again in another land.

But Huni had been his companion for many years. He had been his tutor in youth. He had been his jackal in later days. He had been as near to a confidant as a good king should let any become. And he had been very faithful to him.

Bwene was aware of weakness within himself that shaped his reply: "Well, there is no haste. There is food enough. We will wait awhile, that the leg may heal, as it is likely to do."

He went to Huni, and spoke comforting words.

He went to rest when the night came, in the bed where he had slept all the years that he had been king. Huni lay by the opposite wall. Plini lay at the inner side. The women were in a cave somewhat apart.

Bwene had an evil dream during the night. It was a vision of Gwa, a wife whom he had loved for a few months for her beauty of form, and her quaintness of wit, and her gentle ways. "Lord," she had said, when she had become pregnant by him, "save me from the Queen's eyes." But that had been more than he was able to do. She had disappeared, and he knew not where, though he could guess well that the Queen knew. Now she had come back in the night, in a vivid way which it was not easy to bear.

"It is because," he said to himself, as he lay awake in a dawn which could not enter the cave, "I am about to go from this land, and she will be left alone, which must be a new sadness to her. I may suppose that her grave is near."

He was aroused by a word from Plini, who had risen, and was adjusting the cave. He saw that Plini bent over where Huni lay. He rose, and went to his side.

He looked down at a dead man, and had no doubt what his end had been. He had been smothered in sleep, so that he could have made no sound, or but little, and that too late to avail. He saw that it must have been very silently done.

The two men looked at each other without words, until the King said: "Plini, you should not have done this."

Plini looked at him with his one eye, and his words were not quick to come. The King felt as one who is unjustly accused in a wordless way. Yet it was absurd, for they must each know by whose hand Huni had died, let others think as they would. Then Plini spoke: "No, lord, I should not have done this."

The King could take that as he would. It might be confession of that which Plini could not defend. It could be taken another way. But what could the King do? Should he slay Plini, and be the only man who remained? It was folly to think.

He said: "Well, it is done. He can lie here. It is a quiet grave. He has had a long life, and he prospered well. He may have avoided a leaner time.... We can go now, when the sun is near to descend."

That was the requiem over Huni's grave. They covered him with a coat of skin which they did not need, and in that cave he may still lie.

CHAPTER THIRTY-FOUR

THE King may have slept ill that night, but the Queen's dreams had been worse than his, being such as come to a waking mind when the hours of the night are long.

She had heard with no great surprise that a way had been found to the Sacred Cave, for she had known more of those caves than she was ever likely to say, but it was natural that it should bring old memories back, and they were such as she did not gladly recall.

She knew now how the Old One had been able to come to her side in the night in her own cave, as it seemed that she might also have gone to the King (as perhaps she had?). It had always been a simpler thing to suppose, than to believe that the Old One could walk unseen through the night, as she would have had her believe. But the Old One could have her own way about that, so that she would be active to save her child from a most merciless law.... It was in the law that the fault had lain. It was not in her.... But she must have thought at that time that there was a way to the Sacred Cave, for that was the tale she had told to Gwa, by which she had lured her to easy death.

"It puts," she had whispered, "my own life in your hands when I tell you this. It is how I saved my own child. Would you have it die, should it prove a girl, as it is so likely to be...? If you have courage for such a stake, you must come in the night, and in so secret a way that no one will ever know, and I will take you to Her, by whom all will be so contrived that your child will be safe, be it maid or boy, and when that is assured, you will be able to bear it in better peace.... But if you are seen, they will suspect much at that day, and I may die for the help that I give you now."

And Gwa, timid, frightened of darkness, dreading the caves, trembling at what she did, but made strong by her desire to protect the life that she was to bear, had followed where she had led, with the help of a torch's light, not to the Sacred Cave, which was a way that she did not know, but deep enough into the entrails of earth for the safety of what Bira designed to do.

"Did you suppose," she had asked, with her strong hands round the throat of the weaker girl, "that I would allow your life, being one who might give birth to a son which would have been death to the one I have yet to bear? If a King may have but one son, then his wives should be less than two." She could see yet, by the torch's light, as it had been fixed to the wall—she could see the prayer in the frightened eyes, she could feel the frantic struggle for breath, perhaps for words, which the pressure of those capable hands would not allow her to speak....

And she supposed that they would now have to pass by the pool in which Gwa had been cast, when her futile struggles were done...which held Gwa and another wife who had died for the same cause, in the same way, though she had been drawn with a different lure, being one whom it had been easy to fool....

But it was only of Gwa she thought. The other had been of little account. It had seemed no more than killing a beast that the larder needs. But Gwa had been one that you could not forget in the same way.... Some are like that, having insurgent souls, which are not easy to still. That was the strength of one who had been weak of arm, and gentle of mood. She could still come in the night, both to Bira and to the King.

But Bira was not one whose eyes would fall to the ground, either for the living or for the dead. She faced all in a bold way, and she had a knowledge now that enabled her to meet the spirit of Gwa in a mocking mood, which she had not been able to feel till now, through all these years of a barren womb, for was she not at last with child by the King?

She had been slow to boast of that which might be less than a certain thing: but she was sure now, and she would tell him as soon as they should be clear of these hateful caves. It would be prelude to the commencement of a new time in a new land.... And the end of an evil law, that was surely dead.

She faced the spirit of Gwa, and her own was unrepentant and unashamed. Must there not be life for the strong, and death for those who are frail of body, or faint of heart? She was not of those who will lead their young to an unborn death! (But the spirit of Gwa may have had her own thoughts about that, for the dead see far.) Yet she would feel more assured of the better days that were soon to be, when she should be free of these caves, and this land should be left behind. Then she would tell Bwene that another child would be theirs, and the shadow which had been a darkness between them would move away.

And they were to be held back from this by a man with a festered leg! An old fool who would potter vainly behind the King: who brought no children or wife, nor any strength of his own to the new tribe they would have to be.... They might be here for long weeks till the man should die, or longer yet if his leg should mend in a halting way.

And meanwhile the apes, that were cowering now, in fear of death from the Ho-Tu spears, would recover spirit and move abroad, so that they might become fatal to those who could pass now through the night of a silent land.... She saw Huni as one who brings wreck to all, with no gain to himself, and that because of the maudlin weakness of men—for any woman (or, at least, one with an unborn child, whom it was her part to bring to birth in a safer place) would see that his throat ought to be cut for the common good; and lest he should be left to die of hunger and thirst in a cave that he could not quit.

It was most for that unborn life, being the passion for which she had sinned before, that she rose up in the night, stepping over Tela, who did not stir, and went to do that herself for which the King was too doubtful of heart, though the need was clear.

She did not think that any would wake, for she knew how deep is the sleeping of wearied men, when the midnight is not far past. Huni was the one most likely to be lying with open eyes, and she would think she came as a friend. There would be no outcry from him.... And when he knew what she came to do, it would be a second too late for that.... She did not think that any would wake, for she was not one to fumble at that she had clearly planned. But if they should, she would not be greatly afraid. It was a thing that someone must have courage to do, and she knew that her own worth to the King was much more than that of Huni by any count.... If he were wroth beyond cause, she could tell him that which would turn his thoughts in a new way.... But her hands had been strong, and her knee firm, and Huni's struggles were soon done.... The King and Plini slept on, and she did not know that Tela who slept in a lighter way, had heard her return, and been aware when she stepped over her to find her own place by the wall.... And what of that, if she had? Tela was her own child; and she had the virtue of silent lips.

She would have been right if she had thought that Tela would make no accusation, but it may be supposed that she had had a guess that was true, for when the King said some thing to her at a later hour, by which it seemed that he held Plini as being the cause of his comrade's death, Tela lifted eyes which were bluer than any that had more boldness to front the sun, and said, with the gravity of one using words which are picked with care: "It is ill to judge of that which we do not see."

The King understood that Tela absolved Plini of having any hand in that death, though he was not sure of what she might think beyond that.

"You think well," he said, "of that man."

"So I do. He is much to me."

"Even though he have an eye fewer than most?"

"I have heard that it was lost in a good way."

"That is not denied. Would you say that you are much also to him?"

"Yes. You may say that if you will."

"But you know that, as priestess, you cannot wed?"

"When we are clear of this trap, I will give words to a better thing."

The King pondered this, and was not displeased. He saw that the social order which had been at once a strength and a bondage for all his years, and which he had seen to be far more powerful than he, was now a ruin around their feet. They must win out, if they could, to another time, and perhaps the dreaming of better gods.

CHAPTER THIRTY-FIVE

"I WILL leave the cave closed," the King said, "though it will mean, as I suppose, that it will be entered again by no living thing while the earth endures, except we return, and find entrance the way we now go, or through one of the other caves.

He knew not why he made this resolve, which may have been from no better cause than the instinct that is common to men, that they will be protected behind their backs; but no one spoke in reply, and they went out of the cave into the denser darkness of the tunnels beyond, the torches flickering on the black walls, and Tela leading the way.

The King went next to her, as his right was, with Bira behind, Raina following her, and Plini closing the rear.

Raina had the feeling again which had been frequently hers since the end of the days when they had been alone, Tela and she, that she looked on at a play in which she could take no part, but whether she would have been glad to do so or not was a point that she could not resolve.

They had started while the sun was yet high in the world without, though it was descending the sky, for they had far to go, and wished for a time of rest before they should emerge to the higher land, and after that to have the full length of the night, that they might be far away before the next day should appear.

They must first go by the long way which led back to the Queen's cave, and must be nearly there before they could turn aside at the passage where the Old One had made her sign.

They were about at the point where they must turn to go back when Tela, who talked to the King at times, he being next behind her, said that the pools that they passed, in which the torches would shine as though the water were a surface of polished night, were lower than she could remember to have seen them before.

"But," she added, "there is little wonder in that, for they will ever go up and down as the skies are cloudless without, or have been darkened with frequent rain. They change as the seasons change, and are as fickle as they. There are points we shall reach before we come to the upward climb (from which we are yet far) where we might have waded at times to a good depth, but which will now be entirely dry."

"It matters nought," Bira said from behind, "what there may be upon either hand, so that our eyes be set on the path we take, and the light be cast in the same way. It is no gain to us who must come behind that you cast it about in the way you do."

Tela was surprised at a sharpness of speech which might be frequent enough from the Queen's lips, but was not often addressed to her; but she knew it was true that she had cast the light she carried somewhat far from the path at times, as she had talked with the King.

"I did not suppose," she said, "that you were not lighted enough, and the path is smooth about here, but I will be heedful that you shall have no cause to complain again."

The Queen answered in a more friendly voice, but as one who will keep her point: "It is not all to whom the entrails of earth are as clear as they are to you. For most, if we see the less, we are better pleased, so that we know where our feet are set."

They went on for a time of silence after these words, and at a fair pace for those who were burdened with tools and gear, which were hanged about them so that their arms were left free. And then Tela saw something which lay half out of a pool they passed, which was as low as any of which she had spoken before. She went on, speaking no word, and the King did not observe, and if Bira saw it she gave no sign.

But Plini called from behind: "We should heed that we do not come to some deadly thing. There are a man's bones at your feet."

The King stopped. "What," he asked, "is that you say of a man's bones?"

Tela said: "There is nothing to fear." She would have gone on.

But the King had seen. He stepped down a slope of rock to the water's side.

There was a time when they were all silent before he spoke, while he looked down at the bones.

"Plini," he called, and his voice had the ominous tone of one who has dreadful proof of that he had doubted long, but which he will still not believe till it have been put to a final test, "cast your torch here…. I would see if there be more bones in this pool."

Plini bent at his side. "They are a girl's bones.... She is one who died, as I think, of a broken neck.... There are more bones in the deeper pit." A moment later, Bwene looked down at the bones of another girl, and at a red jewel which was still fastened around her neck.

"This," he said, "is one that I gave to Gwa, on the morning before she could not be found."

"Well," the Queen said, as one who would change the talk to a lighter tone, "she has been long dead. Shall we go on?"

The King looked up, and his eyes were not pleasant to see, though Bira met them without evident fear.

"There may be but four," he said, "when we go on."

The Queen's eyes flinched somewhat at that, but she recovered courage to say: "These are things of a dead time, which we are leaving behind. They are in the grave of years that are past, and you would have done better to turn your eyes in another way, as Tela would have led you to do.... But if you will debate such matters where others hear, do you blame that I wrought so that our daughter is living now, whom you would have let them slay?"

"It is true," he said, "that you saved our child, as may be told to we few who remain after wrath hath smitten the land, and for that I have never blamed you at all. If you did wrong (as we were taught to believe), I said in my heart that it is for the gods, and not me.

"Even when you were cursed that you would not bear, I did not blame you for that; nor even when, as it seemed, the people were cursed alike. I said still, 'it is a matter for gods, not men. It may be they will tire of wrath, or will find a new cause in another land, so that they may leave us alone....' But this is another thing.

"I will have no forgiveness for one who took the lives of the wives I chose, and of my sons who were not yet born."

With this word, he drove the spear in. It was a sudden merciless thrust, and Tela's torch shone on the point, as it came out at the Queen's back. He felt her weight drag on the haft, as she sank, and he pulled it free.

She looked up at him with bitter and mocking eyes. "You have done," she said, and her voice was still level and strong, as though she had not taken a wound from which the blood leapt in the torches' light, "you have done yourself that which you say you cannot forgive. I should have told you in the next word that I am at last bearing your son."

"That is truth?"

"It is one that is told too late."

168

"Plini," he said, "can we staunch the wound?"

"You may try," she said, in a weaker voice, "but you will fail, as you fail in all that you do."

And with those words she went to her own place, which the gods know.

CHAPTER THIRTY-SIX

THE four looked down at the dead, and the King was the first to speak.

"Tela," he asked, "did you know of this before now?"

"Father," she replied, calling him so for the first time, "there were things I knew, and I guessed much. I would have led you on if I could."

"So I saw. But the gods had another will. We may see by this that they neither hasten nor tire."

Tela made no answer to that, and, after a silence, he went on: "Daughter, I have brought myself to a great grief, for the bond of years is not one that can be forgot, and she who lies dead would have been a great queen in a better day.... Will you say I have done wrong?"

Tela's feet were wet with her mother's blood. She was slow to reply. When she spoke, she said: "I can give no answer to that. I would judge none, and last of all those who gave me life, so that I have brought sorrow to them; for, had I died, I suppose these things would not have been as they are. But it must be evil fruit which we pluck from an evil tree, and we were born to lies which, we may hope, are now dead.

"I would say that you did not strike with your own hand, and you would draw it back if you could, knowing what you now do. It was neither your hand nor will. It was the vengeance of Gwa, for which she had waited here."

"Will the water rise to the place where the Queen lies?"

"It will rise beyond that at the next rains, which are now due."

"Then we will leave them to the same tomb."

"I suppose," Tela said, and her voice had the distant sound of one who speaks from a dream, for though she might cast aside all the guile with which the Old One had clothed her pretence of un-earthly power, she could not lose thereby all that had come to herself in the long loneliness of the years, "I suppose they will not be wrathful for that; for they will be friends, now the whole is done."

"It is a good thought," the King said. "We will let them be as they are."

So they went on, leaving the dead, as the living must, and the more so when their own lives are not sure.

But the King would have them go first, so that he stayed for a while, shedding tears which they did not see. Whether they were for Gwa, or for her by whose hand she died, it would not have been simple for him to say, but it is sure that he gave no thought to the third of those who were dead, as is the portion of some.... The torches' light became distant, and stayed.... He went on, seeing that they must have halted for him, and darkness covered the dead.

CHAPTER THIRTY-SEVEN

THEY came out to a place of trees in a deep cleft, and overhead was a narrow ribbon of sky, showing clouded stars, but the moon would not rise till a later hour.

The walls of the cleft were steep, and they moved with what silence they could, seeking a place to climb, and stumbling for lack of light, the torches being put out, lest they should invite those who were less than friends.

When they had gone for too long a time, now seeking among the trees for a spot where they could make ascent, now coming out to the open way that they might progress at better pace, and now drawing back to the trees again as the dark dwellings of the apes made ominous shadows upon the path, Raina became assured that it was that gorge in which she had been confined at the first with those by whom the water had been fetched from the outer cliff, and with this knowledge she guided them, though with doubtful feet, to that place where she had first made her descent, and there they climbed to the upper plain.

Here they met no foe but a cold wind, or so it seemed to those who were used to the heat of the lower land. They looked up to a clouded sky, which had lost the few stars they had seen before. They felt rain. The plain was bare of life, and so level that they could go forward with ease, however dark it might be.

So they did, till they came to the edge of another gorge, at which they must turn aside till they reached its head and go forward again.

They would have been glad of a moon at this time, which would have been of more use than the rain, that they might be aware of the way they went; but the gorges running mainly from east to west, and the mountains they sought to reach being those which they had seen before (except only the King) in the eastern sky, they considered that they might hinder them less than they would guide them aright, and so went on with a better heart.

But when the sun rose at last, showing a pale disc through the clouds, it was well on their left hand, making it plain that they had gone too much in a southerly way. They looked round in a better light, on a scene that was flat and bare, but the yellow growth that Raina had seen at first was turning now to a dusky green, under the caress of the rain, of which there had been much in the last two days, coming in sudden storms, while they had been sheltered within the caves.

They had little comfort in that, or in the distance of the plain which was still to be crossed. They must be content that they saw no apes, and that the rain, for the time, was done. The mountains were still far, and there was no food to be safely sought on that empty plain, the fertile gorges of which must be avoided with care, lest they should rouse a nest of the apes against which they would have had no force to prevail. They had not thought that the mountains would look so far when the dawn should come.

But in the next hour they came to the edge of a cliff which fell far down to the gorge of the great river which was the border of the Ho-Tu land, and they found shelter on the edge of this cliff, where they could rest without urgent fear.

They took food, and, as they sat, Raina found herself at the King's side, if he could still be so called, with kingdom and nation gone. Four are different from five. She did not call herself the King's friend in a close way (though she gave him regard, and was aware at times that he would look at her with more than a casual glance), but she knew that she had lost the feeling, since Bira died, that she was moving among those to whom she did not belong.

Plini's eye was for Tela alone, and her words for him. Raina thought that he should be more than content with that which fortune brought to his door, as, in fact, he was. Gentle, timid-seeming at times, and with the mien of one who would not aggress, Tela had yet shown herself to be quietly sufficient for whatever event might come in a shaking world. The dark, small head, the slender doe-like beauty of form, contained enough of Bira's implacable spirit, enough of Bwene's tolerant wisdom, to fit her for the new adventure of life they were seeking now....

Bwene looked at Raina as though he would speak, but his words delayed. His eyes became distant again. When they returned to her, it still seemed that he had something to say for which the words were not simple to find.

But when he spoke at last, it was in a bold way, as one who had not forgotten that he was king, and though he gave her the high title by which alone she was called, it sounded, as it had done from some others before, to be more of custom than of belief.

"Goddess, you have seen three wives I have had, of whom I slew one, and two had been slain by her, and you are known to my grown child, who will call you friend. Would you be companion to me, or do you look for a better fate?"

She turned to him a gaze that was as direct as his own.

"You mean, by that, that you ask me to be your wife?"

"Yes," he said, "for how else should it be, as we now are?"

She saw reason in that, and she felt that it would be vain to reply that she belonged to another world; for, if so, what did she do here?

He waited with a patient gravity for her reply, but she had seen him to be a man of resolute will, who could be quick to act, even to the giving of death, and she thought that he would be strong to take what was his, in his own time. As though to make the issue clear to herself, he asked again, as she was not quick to reply: "Would you continue with us, or would you go now in your own way?"

"No," she allowed. "I was not thinking to go."

For it was not a thing to be lightly faced in that world, as she now knew it to be. Of their kind, she had found friends. The King had shown, when Swashki would have carried her off, that he would risk something to take her part, though his motive may not have been as simple as that. Now he offered her all he could. If it could be said that he asked a price, it was one that was within right, if she should choose to stay at his side.... Would he let her go, if she should say she had so resolved? It was hard to guess.

She supposed that he did not expect that, seeing her so clearly alone. He might change at such a word to the elemental violence which he would consider the need required. She could not tell, being in a world that was still of such strangeness to her.

She was not even sure of what her own choice would be, except that she had a colder dread of being alone in that hostile world than she would have felt toward one of which she might know less.

With the instinct of delay that is a woman's first weapon at such a pass, she said: "Shall we leave this talk till we are clear of a hateful land, and find a place to remain?"

He looked at her as one who weighs both the meaning of what he hears and what it should lead him to do, but with an eagerness of desire that he was not careful to hide, so that her heart beat in some doubt of what the next moment might bring; but he only said: "It shall be left for this time," and rose in preparation to go.

CHAPTER THIRTY-EIGHT

THEY followed the edge of the cliff for two days, with the great river curving below. They looked across at a lower land, that was green with forest as far as their sight could reach, so that it showed no more than a sea of boughs that fought upward to find the light, over which some birds moved, soaring at times, but seldom to the height at which themselves stood, the trees being very distant below.

They debated that they should descend, and attempt to cross the river, which they supposed that they could swim without much peril in that, but they did not know how far inland the homes of the Ho-Tus might extend under that shelter of trees, and they had heard enough of the Ho-Tu laughter, and seen enough of their spears, one of which Plini still bore, as a spoil that he was reluctant to throw away. He had whittled its wooden haft, in the hope of lightening it to his own strength, till he found that its balance went, so that it would be useless to throw; but he had made it a weapon that he could lift with greater ease than before, and of a more formidable and far more durable kind than the fish-bone spear he had cast aside, which he could not have replaced by the way they had now come, if it should have snapped, as such spears were always likely to do.

They went on, seeing no life beyond that of birds, or small strange creatures of rabbit size. If the apes dwelt in these parts, they did not come up on to the high plain, and if there were any of the canyons that were their homes, they did not open toward the river cliff, but ran in the direction from the mountains toward the sea.

It rained much during these days, and they had a night during which their shelter was poor, so that they had little comfort till they came to a place where the river approached in a great curve from the south, and the cliff, which had been its bank until then, swept back to the north, so that they widened quickly apart.

They stood on the edge of the high land, and looked down to a valley of lava and sterile stone, from the far side of which rose a tier of hills of a barren front, with mountains beyond, which were white with abiding snow.

To go that way did not seem to give a good prospect of life, even though there might be an absence of active foes, for their food was low, and they were not inured to extremes of tempest or cold by the climate from which they came.

They looked to southward, following the river's course, and the mountains were further away. There was a wide space of forest land between the right bank and the rising hills, similar in kind, though less dense than that which had clothed its left bank from the first, and which went southward beyond their sight, even from where they stood to the sea, being the land of the Ho-Tus.

Bwene said: "The Ho-Tus have a great land, without needing to come to this forest which is on the same bank where we now are, and it is a river which, we may hope, they have not wandered to cross, as they left us in peace at its mouth until the apes invaded the land.

"But be that as it may, we must go where food can be had, which is not the way of the barren hills.

"I would cross them with a good will, if we had provision made, and were of equal strength for such toil, and it is that which we may do at a later day, for they must have a far side, where there may be a land that is fertile and empty of men. It may have riches we have not dreamed, as it is natural to hope of a land that is out of sight.... But, for this time, we must go down to the woods, and even if the Ho-Tus be there, we must go south as we are best able to do, passing them in a secret haste, which we must hope that they will not see."

He spoke as one who does not discuss but decides for all, having a life's habit of that. Plini did not deny his right, though he might have said more had he thought it to be less than a good plan. But so he said that it was, in a short word, and the two girls (who had drawn more together since Bira died, so that they were now walking by two and two, and Tela was no longer at Plini's side) said nothing at all, being content enough that the King had chosen to turn from that which had the look of a most barren and arduous way.

So they descended the cliffs, and came, after some hours, to the green of the lower land, where the trees were frequent, but not so that they could not pass freely between, and the undergrowth was not dense, so that they went forward with ease, though they must be wary ever of sight and sound, as men will who enter an unknown place; and the more if it be fruitful, and good to see, for it is likely that there will be those, whether beasts or men, who will have come there before, and think it better to hold than share.

They found fruits which were no less good because they had not met them before, and nuts of excellent kinds, but saw no men, and no beasts but such as were weak and fled, and the flashing of timid wings as they stirred the trees.

It seemed that they had come to a pleasant and empty land, until they looked up to a green platform which made a shadow above their heads, and they withdrew to a thicket's shade, being unsure of what its meaning might be.

"It would seem," Bwene said, "to be the floor of such a house as the Ho-Tus are said to have built in the trees in the ancient days, before they came to dwell on the ground, as they now do. But it has the look of one that is void, as we must hope it to be."

They watched for a time, and then Plini made a cautious circuit about the place, and came back to say: "It is empty, as I suppose; for there is no outcast refuse or filth around, such as marks the dwellings of men, neither is there sign of feet on a trodden path."

"That is near to proof," Bwene replied, "though it may be the home of such as make their way through the boughs, rather than on the ground. But it has been a house of size, though it may be vacant now. If it have been long left, it might be a safety to make it ours."

He said to Plini: "You can come with me, and we will see whether it be vacant or held by those we can face, either in friendship or war; and you," he said to Tela and Raina, "will do better to wait here at the first, and be very ready to run."

They laid down their spears, which would not help them in that ascent, and began to seek where they could climb, having their flint-head clubs hanging against their sides.

CHAPTER THIRTY-NINE

MOROSE, silent, the red ape sat in the high platform within the trees, and as he brooded his great hands moved in a restless desire to be round the throats of those who had cast him out.

He had recovered much of his strength since he had been chased away by the younger males from the community which he had ruled and bullied for more summers than he could remember apart. They went back till they became a blur of recollections which could not be clearly arranged, though, after the manner of all his kind, he would sit for long hours dwelling upon the past, and reconstructing that which had been, as men who toil, or who fill their thoughts with events that they have not seen, will have little leisure to do, losing much of their own lives in those which are further away.

But his thoughts were not now on the distant days of arrogant youth, or of years when none had dared to question his rule. He had been lord of the red apes of the trees, and there had been no male who would not swing quickly aside rather than close his way, no female who would not be proud if he stroked her fur. There had been laws for others, but not for him.

Then there had been one that he had slain, in a sudden passion of wrath, such as had become more frequent in recent years. It was a young ape, not more than half-grown, who had taken food which he had been stretching to have. It was not the first time that such things had been, but this time it had been received in a different way. He had been assaulted at once by a score of those whom he would have brought separately to a sure death, and there could be only one end. He had escaped, by his great strength, when he had been covered with wounds and blood, and had fled blindly and far, to find this refuge within the trees, where he had sat plotting revenge in a futile way, while his wounds had healed.

The red apes were cunning, and very strong. There was none stronger than they. Where they made their homes, even the leopards would leave the land.

This was not their domain, for they were better pleased with the food they found in the woods that mounted the lower slopes of the distant hills; nor were their dwellings alike to this four-chambered platform, with its elaborate over-lacing of boughs which would carry off the heaviest downfall of rain, leaving the inside dry, and unstirred by any outer torment of wind.

This house had been built, as Bwene guessed, by the Ho-Tus of a distant day. For there had been a time when they had invaded the land, thinking it as pleasant and good as any on the left bank of the flood, but a sickness had fallen on those who came, whether from the eating of evil fruit, or a stinging of flies, or some other cause which might be harder to guess, and so they had gone back, and, as the sickness had not pursued, they had called it an evil land, cursed by some unknown god, and had left it alone, having space enough in that they already had, and more to the south, where they could spread as they would, and no sickness came.

So the land had remained empty of men or the greater beasts, lying thus between those of the Ho-Tus and the red apes of the hills, and he who sat and gloomed on that platform now was no more than an exile dwelling apart, and dreaming vengeance beyond his power.

His brooding was not of such a kind as to make him unaware of the forest sounds, and he had lifted a sudden head, and become rigid in his regard, while the four who came had been some distance away.

The tree dwelling was more damaged by weather and time to a near view than it appeared to those who looked up from below. It had gaps in sides and floor through which the red ape could see, though he was not seen.

He considered those who came, and felt a stir of anger mixed with contempt, for he thought them to be of small account, and far weaker than he. But they were four, and he saw two spears which he did not like. He observed that the two whom he judged to be females were unarmed, and he thought that there would be little avail in the strength of their own limbs in a bout of strife, though they might be pleasant to make a spoil.

Now he saw the two men approach to the foot of the upright ladder of steps by which the Ho-Tus had made their ascent.

These steps were strongly made, to support the weight of the Ho-Tus, and so far apart that Bwene found that he must lift his feet high, if he were to go up by that way. He was more content to see that they were choked by the growth of a creeping plant that had long followed its will. He was sure that there had been no recent feet on those steps, for he could not see even a tendril bruised. He was not likely to guess that there was one above who had approached by another way. He went up with confident speed.

The red ape stretched out an arm that was near to his own length, and swung himself out through a window gap in the wall of boughs. Let the men climb. It was the women with whom he would deal the while. Silent and unobserved, he dropped to the ground.

Tela looked round in a green gloom of which she was glad after the light of the last days, for that had vexed her eyes more than she would have been quick to allow. She saw something which moved under the dense shade of a thicket, and which became very still as she looked that way. It was in such shadows that she could see best, and it was of her nature that she made no motion at what she saw. A moment later she said to Raina: "Do not start, or look back, but move slowly toward the spears, as though we wander idly about. There is a great ape in the bushes behind, who is creeping up at our backs."

Raina controlled herself to answer in the same tone: "Is he far behind?"

"He is not yet close. I suppose he aims to creep upon us so that we may not run, or he may know that we have friends who are near."

Raina strolled a few paces aside, and turned to point to the trees in another way. It was hard not to move more quickly at such a need. She asked: "Shall we reach the spears?"

"I cannot tell when he will rush. He has moved nearer twice in a cautious way. If he come, we can move apart, running widely to right and left, and one should reach, if not both. If they would come back!"

But there was no sign from those who had disappeared overhead.

They were close to the spears when the ape leapt. As they lay on the ground, he may not even have noticed that they were there.

"You should take Plini's," Tela had said, "for you are stronger than I."

"Let us snatch them quickly now," Raina replied, "and if he see them, he may move off."

They started forward at that, the weapons not being more than three yards away, at the moment that the ape sprang, making Raina his aim. Her own motion, coming abruptly, caused him to fail in part, so that he did not seize her as he had thought, but bore her down to the ground.

Tela was not slow at her side. She picked up the King's spear, and, though it was strange to her hand, she made a thrust which left a rib bare in a shaggy side, and stained the rust-coloured fur with a brighter red. The slender spear glanced forward from off the rib, and the ape made a snatch at it from which Tela scarcely could draw it clear. She stepped back, well content that he followed her in a new wrath, giving Raina time to rise from the ground.

It was a duel which could have but one end. Tela would have been caught in a dozen yards, had she tried to run. Retreating backward as she did, she kept her far stronger opponent off for some paces, as he dodged the threats of the spear; then, at some cost of blood to his lower arm, he had the spear in his hands, and had snapped it through like a twig. Tela could retreat no more, had she had the time. She felt her back on a tree. It was Raina who gave her the life that she would never be much nearer to lose, repaying, in literal style, the rescue she had had a moment before.

The blade of the heavy Ho-Tu spear, awkwardly as it must be controlled by one to whom its weight was unknown before, did more damage behind his ribs than he had felt from the spear that had gone in from the front. He turned, snarling and fierce, and was stabbed again as he caught the long blade in incautious hands, and found that it differed much from the mere point of bone which had attacked him before. But the next moment he had the haft in a surer grip, and wrenched it from her with such ease that it might have been thought that it was a surrender of willing hands.

As he did so he was distracted again by the shouts of Plini and the King, who came in haste to rescue their women kind. It was a haste which would have been too late had he thought only of dealing death, and of flight thereafter from those who could not have followed among the boughs. But, as he looked at Raina, the lust of possession entered his heart, and he thought, in contempt of the wounds he had, that he would seize and bear her away.

Seize her he did, with a savage bruising strength that made her struggles as futile as those of a lamb in the butcher's grip but as he walked he was leaving a trail of his own blood which must have degraded his might, and he was of less strength through his wounds of a month ago. He found (as his full vigour might not have done) that she was too great a weight for him to bear upward among the trees. But he did not therefore resign his prey. He put her down, and turned to deal with those two who made their foolish advance, without even showing such spears as had annoyed him before.

He might have done better for himself had he caught up the Ho-Tu spear which he had flung away as he wrenched it from Raina's hands. His cunning would have been quite enough for him to have put it to deadly use, but he was accustomed to rely on the strength of his terrible hands, and habit prevailed, as it is likely to do at such crises of passion and strife.

Plini, being the swifter upon his feet, was the first to come up. He found that his club was of no avail, unless he would risk himself within reach of the long arms of the ape. He drew back, seeking to make play till he should have the support of the King. The ape thought it best for himself that he should end one foe at a time. There was some dodging, and a rush from which Plini slipped adroitly aside, aiming a blow that fell short. He feinted again, and got a blow home. He thought that he had come clear from that, but a backward sweep of the ape's arm struck him with such force that he was lifted from off the ground, and flung against a near tree, where he fell, and was slow to rise.

By now, Bwene was close. He saw what had been, and thought that there was but one chance, and that poor, or the ape would have his will with them four, which would have been the end of the hopes they had.

He rushed boldly in, disregarding how his foe might return the blow which he brought down on the snarling face.

It was a kingly stroke, and such a club may not have been used in a better way. It struck fully between the eyes, the jagged flint crushing into the skull: it came down on the forward length of the face, so that the snout was streaming blood, as the huge arms closed about him in a grip which he could not break.... It would have been death for death, had there not been two women's hands on the haft of the Ho-Tu spear, as it was driven in from behind....

The four looked round on the fair green woods: they looked down on the dead.

"He had been alone," the King said, "and he had been here but a short time, by the signs which we had noticed above. He has scars of wounds which he must have taken from many, but weaker, hands; it may be a moon ago. I should say that he has been thrust out by his kin, and has wandered to lonely woods.

"It is here, in a fairer land than we knew before, that we have had our first fight, and prevailed. It is here we have fought as one"—he looked at Raina as he said this, in a way she must understand—

"and it is here as one we will stay, that we may build, it may be, a better race than that which we were before, such as will not fly from the apes of the higher lands, nor fear the laugh of the Ho-Tus, and will have better customs than they."

He spoke as a king speaks, deciding for all, and he looked at Raina so that she knew that the time had come when she must elect to be Bwene's bride, or walk in her own way, if that should not be more than they would permit her to do.

There was a silence when the King ceased, in which she was aware of the forest sounds, and a stir of wind in the trees, and it seemed that it went on long, while she knew it was time to speak, and was still unsure what the words would be.... And then knew that that pause of doubt was all the assent that the King required.